ON THE CASE

When her Great Uncle Ronald dies, Megan Walters inherits his half of a detective agency. However, the other half is owned by the sullen Josh Rayne, whose main aim is to buy her out. Meanwhile, though, they must work together. As they attempt to track down a client's long-missing aunt, in the hope of persuading her to be tested for a bone marrow transplant match, Megan and Josh find themselves warming to each other . . .

ENID REECE

◆

ON THE CASE

Complete and Unabridged

LINFORD
Leicester

First published in Great Britain in 2021

First Linford Edition
published 2022

A catalogue record for this book is available
from the British Library.

ISBN 978–1–4448–4937–0

Published by
Ulverscroft Limited
Anstey, Leicestershire

Printed and bound in Great Britain by
TJ Books Ltd., Padstow, Cornwall

This book is printed on acid-free paper

1

Megan said, 'Could you repeat that, please?' at the same time as the man sitting opposite her rose from his chair and shouted, 'No, that's not possible!'

Josh Rayne was angry. His brown eyes darkened and he banged his fist on the table. Megan gripped the arms of her chair. Heavens above this man did not like hearing bad news.

'Calm down, Mr Rayne,' Mr Hibbs, the solicitor, said, keeping his voice steady. 'It's no good losing your temper.'

Josh glared at the other man for a moment before sitting down. Megan breathed a sigh of relief and wondered what she'd walked in on.

She'd received the letter from Parish and Hibbs Solicitors requesting her presence. She didn't know what it was about but was curious to find out. A quick call to the solicitors wasn't very informative apart from that it was something to do with the will of her Great Uncle Ronald Merriweather, a man she'd only a vague memory of from childhood.

She would have asked her mother but she was away on holiday and couldn't be contacted until her return later that day.

It turned out that she'd been left his half of a detective agency. The man opposite her owned the other half and was now her partner and he was not happy about it, not one little bit.

'I'll contest it,' Josh Rayne said. Mr Hibbs looked at him over his glasses. 'You can certainly try, but I doubt it will do you much good. Mr Merriweather was of sound mind when he made out his will.'

Josh looked over at Megan. 'Did you know?' he said through gritted teeth.

She shook her head.

'Do you know anything about running a detective agency?'

'Not a thing,' she admitted.

'Well, you're not going to be much good then, are you?' He glared at her.

How rude, thought Megan, glaring

2

back at him. 'I won't know until I try,' she retorted.

Up until that moment, she'd no intention of having anything to do with the detective agency but this man annoyed her. Who did he think he was? He didn't know her. Didn't know what she did. In an instant, she decided that she would accept the contents of her Great Uncle's will.

She stood up. 'Thank you, Mr Hibbs.' She shook his hand and turned to the other man who, somehow through no fault of her own seemed to think of her as an enemy. She took in his handsome features as his dark brown eyes bored into her blue ones. If he imagined he could intimidate her he was sadly mistaken.

'I'll be in touch,' she said turning her face away from him. The solicitor handed her a copy of the will. Keeping her temper in check she walked out of the room and quietly shut the door.

She walked out of the solicitor's office and got into her car before letting out a huge sigh of relief. What had she done? What did she know about detecting anything? Up until two weeks ago, she'd worked at Petal Power, a small flower shop by the station. The only thing she'd detected was how different flowers went together to make a spectacular bouquet. Unfortunately, the owner decided to retire and the shop was sold to another family who didn't need Megan's services, so she was out of work.

This opportunity was probably too good to resist — plus she quite liked the idea of irritating Josh Rayne. So far he hadn't relayed one kind word to her. OK, she acknowledged it was a bit of a shock for him but why take it out on her? She was an innocent in all this.

She turned on the engine and pulled away into the traffic. Thank goodness her mother would be home this evening and she could talk to her about it. Particularly, why on earth a Great Uncle that she hardly remembered and only met a couple of times would leave her anything.

★ ★ ★

Josh Rayne stood in the doorway of the solicitors' office and watched as Megan Walters drove off down the road. What a mess, he mused and why had Ronald never mentioned his intentions?

Ronald's death was quick. Being a large man he'd never really bothered to look after himself and a sudden heart attack was unexpected.

Josh's father had been the original partner in the business, but after his death, he'd left his son his half of the agency. Josh liked a challenge and he saw the outdated business as something he could get his teeth into. He wanted to expand the business and he was so sure that if anything happened to Ronald, the older man would have left his half share to Josh. They'd got on well and it was a total shock when Mr Hibbs had read out the will.

Josh didn't even know about Ronald's relations.

He certainly never mentioned any

family and no one ever visited him as far as he was aware.

His first thought when Mr Hibbs read out the will was that he could buy this woman's share but that idea was dashed when he remembered the rather large loan he'd just taken out to update the computer system and other necessary equipment that the business desperately needed. There was no other option. He'd just have to put up with her for the time being.

He rubbed the back of his neck — what an absolute mess.

* * *

That evening Megan welcomed her mother home from her recent cruise, and they settled down with a cup of tea and a plate of biscuits ready for a long chat. Joyce Walters began to relate tales of her latest excursion when Megan interrupted her with her own news.

'He was always fond of you,' Joyce said as Megan's tale unfolded.

'Really? I don't remember much about him to be honest, apart from him being a big man with an enormous laugh who gave me money for sweets.'

'No, I'm sure you don't,' her mother said, 'Although he was quite fond of you when you were small.' She laughed. 'He said you had a very enquiring mind. You were always asking him questions.'

'Why did he stop coming to see us?'

Her mother pondered the question. 'If I remember rightly he'd rowed with my father. Uncle Ronald was always a bit of an adventurer as I recall. He'd done all sorts of stuff, travelled the world but never really settled down. Anyway, he decided to open up this detective agency in Keatbury, My father decided it was a complete waste of time and told my Uncle so. Words were spoken and we never saw him after that.'

'What I still can't understand is why he left me his half. I mean, he never kept in contact with us. I would have thought that this man, Josh Rayne, would be a better prospect to receive his half of the business.'

'How did he take the news?

Megan took a sip of her tea. 'Not good. From what I gather, he was as surprised as I was about the will, and I'm convinced he doesn't want me as a partner.'

'So, what are you going to do?

'To be honest I wasn't going to do anything but he was just so obnoxious that I told him I'd be in touch.' She shrugged before continuing. 'With me losing my job I might as well give it a go. Plus . . .' she paused for a moment, not meeting her mother's questioning gaze, '. . . it would be good to get away at the moment.'

Her mother sat forward in her chair and studied her daughter. 'Marcus?'

She sighed and looked at her mother. 'I did think he was the one. Just goes to show that I'm no good at picking Mr Right. I'm still not sure how it went so wrong so quickly.'

Megan put down her tea and closed her eyes, thinking back to their first meeting.

She'd met Marcus Rowland when he'd come into the shop looking for flowers for his mother's birthday. They got chatting, discussed the type of flowers his mother liked and after deciding on a bouquet he'd asked her out. He appeared to be fine at the beginning. Tall, good looking and dressed well, a good job in the sales department of a large construction company. They'd gone out for about six months and she was beginning to think that it might turn into something more when the relationship suddenly turned sour.

It was one evening when she'd arranged to meet him at his flat. They were planning on going to see a film. Marcus wasn't quite ready and seeing his laptop open on the coffee table she decided to use it to send an email to a friend. Marcus came into the room just as she sat down and seeing her looking at the screen became angry, accusing her of spying on him. He snapped the laptop shut as she tried to explain but he wouldn't listen. It ended with them having a blazing row about trust and her walking out. Still angry with him the next morning she'd sent him a text telling him that their relationship was over. They hadn't spoken to each other since.

'He wasn't right for you. I always felt that.' Her mother's words cut into her thoughts.

Megan raised an eyebrow. 'You never said.'

'I was hoping you would come to that conclusion yourself. Don't waste any more time thinking about him. Plenty more fish in the sea.'

No, she was over men for the foreseeable future. 'I think I'll concentrate on my new venture for the time being.'

'Good idea. My daughter, the detective. Whatever next?' Her mother shook her head

Megan laughed. 'It will certainly be a challenge, although I don't think Josh Rayne thinks so. Did I mention that not only has Great Uncle Ronald left me half of the business but there's a flat above the office that belonged to him, so I have somewhere to live.'

'Goodness, he must have done well to have a flat as well. From what I remember he never had two pennies to rub together.'

'He must have turned a corner and made money because from what I understand he owned the whole property. The house was converted into two flats and his partner, who I believe was Josh Rayne's father paid half the value of the bottom flat when they went into business together so that they could turn it into an office.'

Joyce drained the rest of her tea and put her hands in the air. 'Honestly I go away for a couple of weeks and when I come home my daughter is part owner of a business and owns a property! Things must be looking up.'

'I'm not sure if it will work out but I'm not going to let Josh Rayne get the better of me.' There was a determined note in her voice. 'I might not know anything about the detective business but

I'm willing to learn.'

'That's my girl,' her mother said. 'When do you think you'll leave?'

Megan looked over at her mother. 'There's nothing to keep me here apart from you. So I think I'll pack up over the next couple of days and then head off. Luckily it's only about twenty miles away from here so I won't be far away.'

Joyce looked sad for a moment. 'I'll miss you.'

'It's not far. We'll still be close to each other,' Megan pointed out, reaching out and squeezing her mother's hand.

'Of course, and I can visit you.' Joyce smiled and changed the subject. 'Now let me tell you about my holiday.'

Megan sat back and listened to her mother wax lyrical about her recent cruise and the people she'd met. Megan often wondered whether she would remarry. Megan's father died when she was fourteen and she'd never seen her mother with another man. She asked her once if she ever felt lonely without having a man in her life. Her mother laughed and told her that she was quite happy as she was, doing what she wanted to do when she wanted to do it without having to check with a partner.

★ ★ ★

Two days later Megan looked around the bedroom that was hers since the day she was born. She'd packed most of her belongings. Just a few reminders of her childhood and teenage years remained. A poster of a popular pop group hung on the wall, a bit tattered at the edges where she'd run her fingers along the face of the lead singer whom she'd crushed on when she was fifteen. The way his dark hair flopped across his forehead reminded her of Josh Rayne.

She pulled herself up short. Why would she compare the two?

All she could remember of the man she'd met was the anger and perhaps despair and frustration that was visible on his face. A small part of her felt sorry for him but there was nothing she could do. She needed a job. He would just have to put up with her for the time being until she decided if she would keep her half of the business or sell it on. Was she making the right decision or should she just give up the idea and let Josh Rayne have the business? Only time would tell. After all, what did she have to lose?

2

Megan phoned ahead advising Josh the day and time of her arrival. There was no answer so she left a message. After a tearful farewell with her mother and promises to telephone every day she set off. 'Anyone would think I was moving to the moon,' she said as she gave her mother one last hug.

'It feels like it,' her mother admitted, her voice trembling a little. 'Anyway I'm allowed to miss my only child when she goes out into the world on her own.'

'Think of all the freedom it will allow you,' Megan teased. Although they'd never lived in each other's pockets she could understand how she felt. It would be strange not seeing her mother each morning or kissing her goodnight as she headed for bed in the evening.

As she drove down the road she wondered what awaited her. No doubt she was going to get another frosty reception, but she wasn't bothered, she could hold her own against anybody.

Knowing nothing about detective agencies she'd gone online to check what exactly a private detective did. It was mostly background checks, spousal problems and the occasional work for government authorities such as the DSS. Josh didn't appear to be a Sam Spade or anything like that, although she could be wrong!

Keatbury was larger than her own home town with Regency and Victorian houses surrounding a large shopping centre. She passed a couple of large parks with children's play areas along with plenty of room for dog walkers. She pulled up outside a row of two storey 19th century houses just off a main road. A plaque hung on the brickwork: *Merriweather & Rayne Investigators.* That would have to change if she stayed. She pushed open the front door to find herself in a small hallway with a couple of chairs either side of a green painted door. At the end of the corridor was a staircase which she assumed led to her living quarters.

There was a note on the door:

Miss Walters.

Have gone out. Make yourself comfortable. Will be back as soon as I can.

He'd scrawled his signature at the bottom. At least he knew she was arriving today.

Megan pushed the door open and walked inside. She'd imagined a dusty, messy office with dark furniture and old fashioned typewriters. She as surprised to see how modern the office was, with two wooden desks with what looked like a new computer on each one. A printer stood in one corner alongside a photocopier and three filing cabinets.

The only thing she was right about was the state of the office. There was paperwork everywhere, piles of folders stacked haphazardly on top of each other ready to fall onto the floor at any moment. She ran her fingers along the top of a tray of letters piled so high it looked like they'd not been attended to in a while. Another tray contained a pile of bills. If there was anything Megan couldn't stand was a slovenly room. She itched to start tidy up but held back, doubting that Josh Rayne would appreciate her doing anything until they'd talked.

She noted a small kitchen area in the corner, a couple of mugs, a pack of tea and a jar of coffee stood on top of a small fridge. Deciding she might as well make herself a cup of coffee while she waited for Josh, she opened the fridge door and pulled out a bottle of milk which looked as though it was a few days old. Perhaps a visit to a shop was in order. She'd seen one of those mini marts at the bottom of the road and headed out.

Josh was still absent from the office when she returned so she made her coffee and helped herself to a couple of biscuits from the pack she'd bought. She sent a quick text to her mother: *Arrived safely. Will ring later*.

She sat down at the desk with a view of the door so she could see anyone who entered the office. There was a diary on the desk and she started glancing through it. She came to today's date and in bold black writing was the word JIMMY. Not even a note to say she was arriving. Josh Rayne certainly didn't want her anywhere near the business if he couldn't even acknowledge her arrival. She leafed through the rest of the diary when she heard the door open.

'Seen anything that interests you?'

She looked up but didn't close the diary. Josh Rayne stood in the doorway. He didn't look happy if the glare on his face was anything to go by.

'Just wondered if you made a note of where you were,' she said, tapping the open diary. 'I would have rung you but I haven't got your number.'

He stared at her and she stared back. She was determined that he wasn't going to intimidate her. She was way past any man doing that.

'I was working, and by the way that's my desk you're sitting at.'

She very nearly told him that there was another desk in the office but decided it was best if she didn't antagonise him any further. She wanted this to work. She wasn't sure how but she was determined.

She said nothing but picked up her coffee and walked to the other desk. 'This OK? She said, sitting down and making herself comfortable.

He didn't go to his desk, but instead walked over to the kettle and made himself a drink, checking the milk before pouring it into the mug.

The silence was unnerving but she stood her ground just sipping her own drink and nibbling on a biscuit.

'The milk was sour so I went a bought some more. Help yourself to a biscuit,' she said, deciding to break the silence.

He grunted and took a sip.

Was that a thank you?

She felt his eyes on her as he finally walked over to his desk, sat down and started rifling through some paperwork.

Oh, so it was going to be an 'ignore Megan and she'll go away day' was it? No, she was not going to let that happen!

'Look,' she said, putting down her

mug. 'I know you don't want me here but unfortunately, my Great Uncle left me part ownership of this business and I intend staying for a long time, so I'd appreciate it if you didn't ignore me and could be little more civil.' There was ice in her voice but she was fed up with his attitude. The journey to the Keatbury had taken longer than she expected due to heavy traffic and she still needed to check over the flat above the office and settle in. 'I know you're frustrated about what happened but it's hardly my fault.'

He didn't respond for a moment, just gazed into his mug before giving a huge sigh. 'You're right, I don't like it and for the life of me I can't understand why Ronnie did this to me.'

There was a tightness in his voice and she almost felt sorry for him.

'You didn't have a clue?'

He shook his head. 'Not one.'

He stared into space for a moment before looking directly at her. 'OK, we'll see how it goes. You probably won't like it. It can be boring and repetitive most of the time.' He gave a hint of a smile that changed his dark features and a dimple appeared at the side of his mouth.

Megan inwardly sighed. Thank goodness. She didn't fancy a continuing frosty atmosphere.

'So, how about you telling me a little bit about what exactly a private detective does?'

He shrugged. 'Nothing really interesting. Background checks mostly, divorces, doing quite a lot of work for local authorities to see if anyone is defrauding them. That's where I've been this morning. Trying to get evidence against a chap I'm sure is claiming benefits he's not entitled to.'

'Did you catch him out?'

'No, unfortunately. He's been giving me the slip for weeks now.' He gave a frustrated sigh.

'Is his name Jimmy by any chance?' Her lips twitched at the look of surprise that appeared on his face. 'His name was in the diary,' she explained.

'A slippery character if ever I saw one,

but I'll catch him.' There was a determined note in his voice and Megan was in no doubt that he meant what he said.

'So how can I help? I might not know the ins and outs of the business but I'm willing to learn.'

Josh studied her for a moment. 'Look, I must warn you now that I will try and buy you out. I can't at the moment because I've just shelled out on all this new office equipment.' He waved a hand around the room. 'To be honest I'd rather work alone — no offence, but I've been doing it for so long I prefer it that way.

'Great Uncle Ronald didn't help?'

Josh scoffed. 'Ronnie? Help? You must be joking! He spent most of his time in the pub after my father died.'

'I can imagine that would have been frustrating,' she said dryly.

'You can say that again. I was lucky my father showed me how the business worked or I wouldn't have known what to do.'

'You've always worked here?'

He shook his head. 'Not full time, no.

I helped out in the office when I was home from university and then started here full time. When Dad got sick and my mother couldn't cope I must admit I took my eye off the ball and left Ronnie to run the business.' He shook his head. 'A big mistake on my part.'

She looked at him, surprised.

'He wasn't in the office most of the time. Ronnie was a sociable kind of person, his idea of drumming up business was to spend his time in the pub chatting to his mates. Not a good combination in my opinion.'

Megan began to feel uncomfortable on hearing how her great uncle operated and could now understand a little why her grandfather fell out with him.

She pushed back her chair 'How about I go and look at the flat above the shop and settle in. We can talk about the business in the morning.'

'Fine,' he said, finishing his coffee and pushing back his own chair. 'I must warn you not to expect too much. As I've already said Ronnie spent most of his time in the pub but at least it's clean. I arranged for a women come in after Ronnie died.'

'That was kind of you,' she said, pleased that he'd been so thoughtful.

'Not kind at all. I was planning on moving in myself. As you know I was certain he'd left me the whole lot. I didn't know there was any family.' His voice turned cold again.

'Oh.' She felt a little deflated that she'd come to the wrong conclusion but she couldn't blame him if his expectations weren't fulfilled.

'I'm sorry about that. Shall we go?' For some reason she needed a break from Josh and his problems.

He pulled out a drawer and reached into it, rifled about and produced a ring of keys. 'Follow me,' he said and walked out of the door.

The flat was small — a kitchen diner, living room with a shower room and bedroom. The furniture was a bit shabby, but looked comfortable. She didn't fancy sleeping in the bed as the mattress sagged and she decided that the first thing she would do was buy a new one. She'd just have to put up with it for a few days.

'As I said. A cleaner as gone over the flat so it's clean. Not sure if you want to change anything. Ronnie left some paperwork but I've not gone through it yet. I suppose you'll want to do it now, being a relative and all that.'

'So there was no second will hidden away then?' she said, trying to inject a little humour into the situation. She was rewarded with a tiny tug at the corner of his lips.

He arched an eyebrow. 'Not that I know of but if you find one let me know. As I've already said I haven't gone through his private paperwork.'

'I'll check all the books, just in case he used it as a marker.'

He chuckled. Megan gave a sigh of relief. He did have a sense of humour after all.

'Right, I'll leave you to it. See you in the morning,' he said, briskly, reverting to his all business manner. He turned towards the door, then halted. 'Almost forgot.' He handed her the bunch of keys. 'For both the office and the flat. Front door key is the largest.' With that he left without as much as a goodbye.

She flopped on the sofa feeling as though she'd been through the mill with the man. At least they'd come to a compromise, although she doubted very much if their truce would last for long. He seemed a determined sort of person, much like herself. She was sure they would clash from time to time. She grinned. She was quite looking forward to the battles ahead.

She checked her watch. Half the day was gone already and she needed to sort her belongings. She bought a few groceries with her but tomorrow she would have to do a bigger shop

She headed downstairs and as she passed the office door she could hear the muffled voice of Josh on the telephone.

Three hours later her suitcases were unpacked, and she settled herself down on the sofa and rang her mother.

'So, how's it going?' were her mother's first words. 'Has Josh Rayne calmed down yet?

Megan smiled. Trust her mother to get straight to the point. 'Not quite, but I suppose I can't blame him. Ronald didn't have much to do with the business after Josh's father died. Left the everyday running to Josh.'

'Sounds like Ronald. He was always one to let others do the work after the initial set up. I'm not surprised. What's the place like? Nice flat is it?'

Megan went on to give her mother a report on the flat and the building.

'Can't wait to see it.'

Megan laughed. 'You sound as though you're missing me already.'

'Darling, I miss you every day, but I would never stop you having a fulfilling life.'

That was one thing she liked about her mother. She was an independent woman and she brought Megan up to be exactly the same. She encouraged her in everything she did.

'Right, I'm going to leave you to it. Ring me tomorrow and let me know how you get on. My daughter, a private detective!' She chuckled. 'I still can't get my head around it.'

Megan laughed. 'Hardly a private detective, Mum. I have a lot to learn first. That's if Josh will teach me and to be honest I have my doubts.'

'Don't be too hard on him. He'll come round. Look, must dash. I'm checking the internet for my next cruise.'

Megan wasn't surprised, her mother loved her cruises. 'OK, I'll leave you to it. I can't believe you're looking into arranging your next holiday. You've only just got back.'

'I know, but one can never book too early. Speak soon.'

Megan cooked herself a meal on the small stove and began to imagine what it would be like to be a lady detective. Would she ever be in danger, or would it be as Josh indicated — just dull, boring, repetitive work? Whatever it turned out to be she was excited at the prospect.

3

Josh was at his desk when Megan entered the office the next morning. He looked up but didn't acknowledge her, just went back to whatever he was doing on his computer.

Ignoring me, are you? she thought to herself. Not going to happen!

She went over to his desk and stood over him, her arms folded. 'Look, Josh. We've been through this. Ignoring me won't make it go away, so let's try to get on and at least be civil shall we?'

He said nothing for a moment and then sighed. 'OK.' He pushed back his chair and looked up at her and then around the office. 'I could do with some help in here,' he admitted, looking around the office. 'Nothing very exciting, I'm afraid, but if you want a wage it has to be done. I was thinking about hiring a girl to run the office when Ronnie died. Paying out two wages is bad enough but I don't think we could run to three.'

'Money that tight?'

'A bit,' he admitted, 'Although it would help if I have time to get the invoices out to customers.' He waved a hand around the office. 'But as you can see clerical work isn't my forte.'

'OK, let that be my first job. I used to do all the invoices and bill paying at the flower shop where I worked, I'm sure I could sort this lot out without too much trouble.'

'Be my guest. How are you with computers? There's an accounting package which is quite easy to use.'

He stood up and walked over to the other desk and switched on the computer. Pressing a few buttons, the accounts package appeared and he patiently explained how it worked.

'I think I've got it, but first I think I'll sort through this mess.' She tapped the overflowing paperwork in one of the trays. 'Hopefully by the end of the day I'll be able to get some invoices posted out to fill our bank account.'

Josh gave a small laugh. 'Don't be too impressed with it. Bank details are on the computer as well.' He rummaged in his desk draw and pulled out a small notebook. 'Here are all the passwords you'll need.'

'Thanks. Look, if it's that bad on the money front I have some savings I can live on for a while.'

His eyes widened and he gave her a look of surprise before shaking his head. 'No, it's fine.' He mentioned an amount. 'Will that be OK for starters? It's the same as I take out for myself.'

'Really?' she said. It was such a small amount. she could manage on it only because she wasn't going to have to pay to rent a flat but how on earth did Josh manage?

He must have read her mind. 'I live with my mother. She didn't cope very well when Dad died so I decided to stay with her. When Ronnie passed away the plan was that I would move into the flat. Of course, that's not possible now.' That bitter note that sometimes crept into his voice appeared again.

She decided to ignore that comment. 'Look on the bright side as soon as the accounts are up to date things will get better. Right, before I start how about a cup of coffee? You can tell me something about the running of the office.'

Over coffee he described the filing system, such as it was. The customer files in the overflowing red tray needed invoicing, there were fewer ones in the blue tray which Josh explained were pending. The two filing cabinets held information of current and historical cases along with customer's names and addresses. These he explained he wanted to upload onto the computer, but once again there'd been no time. She assured him she could handle that which got a small smile out of him.

She pulled a pair of reading glasses from her bag, gave a deep sigh at the challenge ahead, and began to sort the chaos out.

★ ★ ★

Two hours later Josh pushed back his chair and stood up. 'Right I'm off out. Got to catch a man.'

'Sounds exciting.'

'Hah, you must be joking, Jimmy Donaldson is as slippery as they come. He reckons he can't work because of a bad back. Been on social security for over two years but the DSS — our customer, by the way, thinks he's fit to work and they've asked me to prove it.'

'He's the one you were trying to catch yesterday?'

He rubbed the back of his neck. 'He seems to know whenever I'm about. Uses a walking stick although he's notched it up a bit over the last couple of weeks and has started to use a mobility scooter.'

'Perhaps he's a genuine case.'

Josh scoffed. 'Not even a little bit! Anyway I can't stop chatting, must get on. I have a feeling today might be my lucky day. See you later.'

He went to open the door but she called him back. 'What if I need to contact you?' 'Oh, yes we'd better swap mobile numbers I suppose.' He reached into his pocket and pulled out his phone as Megan picked hers up from her desk and they quickly swapped numbers.

'Text me if it's not urgent. My phone's always on silent when I'm on surveillance but I do check for any messages.'

Megan nodded and turned back to her computer. Over the past hour Josh seemed a bit more amenable. Perhaps he was getting used to the idea of having a new partner? She hoped so. There was nothing worse than not getting on with someone you were going to work closely with.

She heard the front door close and looked around her. It was going to take some time but she'd get the office into shape. She picked up a pile of paperwork that needed filing and slowly began to sort through the pages separating them into piles.

The morning went swiftly by and she was surprised how much she'd accomplished. Josh was right when he said he wasn't much to the clerical work. There were letters going back over a year ready to be filed, small notations were on each one referring to one case or another. It certainly looked as though for a long time this was a one man operation with her late great uncle doing nothing to help. She almost felt sorry for Josh. The pressure he must have been under. She was determined to do her bit and get the business back on its feet.

Her stomach grumbled. She checked her watch and realised it was lunchtime. Still no Josh. There'd been no phone calls. In fact, the office was quiet all morning. She hoped that it wasn't always the case. She picked up her bag and switched on the answerphone after deciding to find some lunch. She'd noticed a café in the next street the day before. Hopefully it sold more than coffee and cakes. She also needed to buy some groceries but decided that could wait until later. She was in luck, the café offered cooked meals. As she waited in the queue she looked around her surroundings.

The café wasn't a big building, about

a dozen tables, mostly full at this time of day. A young girl was serving drinks and chatting away as she served, with an older woman, probably in her late twenties, preparing food. The offerings were good and she decided on a latte along with a cheese and tomato Panini. Settling herself down at a table by the window she pulled out her phone and sent a quick text to her mother: *Day 1 — not bad will ring you later*. It was no good ringing her she was at work all day and her boss didn't like her to take private calls in the office.

'Here you are.'

Megan looked up to see the older woman holding out her order. 'Thanks.'

'Any time. I haven't seen you in here before. Just visiting?' the woman asked as she set everything on the table.

Megan shook her head. 'No, I've just moved here. I'm living around the corner.'

'Didn't think I'd seen you before. I only get regulars in here usually. We're a bit off the main thoroughfare of the town centre, although business isn't too bad as long as I keep my prices low. I have Stacey over there to help me with the lunchtime rush. So what do you do? I'm Sarah, by the way.' She held out her hand.

The woman seemed to want to chat and Megan didn't mind. It would be nice to make a few friends. 'Megan,' she said shaking Sarah's hand. 'I'm working at Merriweather and Rayne,' she said.

Sarah looked surprised. 'Josh's place?'

Megan raised an eyebrow before picking up her coffee and taking a sip. 'You know him?'

'For years. Nice chap and so dishy.'

Sarah rolled her eyes and Megan couldn't help but laugh. She supposed he was quite good looking with his dark hair and almost black eyes and the dimple that appeared occasionally when he smiled — although he didn't do much of that.

'So what are you doing, running the office for him?' Sarah asked.

Megan shook her head. 'No, I'm his

partner.' If it was possible Sarah's eyes opened even wider and Megan hastened to put her straight. 'Partner, as in business only.'

'Really? I'm surprised he's taken on a partner. I got the impression the business was his after Ronnie passed away.'

'Ronnie, or rather Ronald, was my great uncle and he left me his share of the business.'

'Really?' Sarah pulled out a chair and plonked herself down. 'Do tell me all the juicy details!'

Megan couldn't help but laugh. Sarah was going to be a breath of fresh air, even if she was bit nosy.

'I hope chatting with me isn't going to get you into trouble with your boss?'

Sarah waved the suggestion away. 'I am the boss, so it's OK.' She looked around the café. 'As you can see, the lunchtime rush is over. Just the clearing up to do. Stacey can managed most of that.' She looked over at the young girl who was engrossed with the screen of her mobile phone. 'When she's not gossiping with her friends.'

She called over to the young girl who looked up with a guilty expression on her face and quickly put her mobile into her pocket and went back to work. Sarah shook her head. 'She's a good worker as long as she concentrates. Never without that mobile phone.'

Megan wasn't surprised when half an hour had passed and Sarah knew everything she needed to know.

'I must get going,' Megan said, gathering her belongings. 'I think I've left the office long enough.'

'Nice chatting with you,' said Sarah. 'Pop in tomorrow and tell me how you're getting on.'

Megan gave her a wave and hurried back to work. Everything was quiet. The desk opposite hers was empty and the answer machine was silent. She decided to send Josh a text. Hopefully he would answer quickly.

There were a few files on his desk but he'd told her under no circumstances should she touch anything. He knew where everything was and didn't want anything disturbed.

Another hour passed and there was still no reply from her text. She wondered if he would ever return, when she heard the front door open. Either a customer or Josh. It was the latter and when he walked into the office she could only stare and then burst out laughing.

'What on earth has happened to you?' she asked, her eyes sparkling with merriment. She tried to school her features but it was difficult. His clothes were covered in mud and leaves and twigs stuck to his trousers, jacket and hair. He could have been mistaken for a scarecrow. The idea made her laugh even harder.

He ran a hand through his hair and scowled. 'It isn't funny,' he growled before picking a few leaves off his coat sleeves.

Megan clenched her jaws together and took a deep breath. He was angry and it was no good antagonising him further.

'Care to tell me what happened?'

Josh said nothing for a moment as he

busied himself picking leaves and twigs off his clothing.

'Jimmy Donaldson, that's what.' He spat the words out as he tried to clean himself up. He looked up at her expecting her to say something but she remained quiet. She was waiting for further information. He took a deep breath, sighed and began his tale.

'Jimmy decided to use his mobility scooter this morning. I followed him at a distance hoping to catch him up to no good.'

'Like what?'

He shrugged. 'Well, I don't know. Picking up a piano and holding it above his head. Something that should be beyond his capabilities.'

Megan's eyes widened. 'He'd hardly pick up a piano on his own.'

'I know that,' he snapped, 'But you know what I mean. I was just using that as an example. Look, do you want to hear the story or not?' He walked over to the kettle and began making a drink.

She put out a hand. 'Sorry, carry on.'

He seemed to be at the end of his tether. She knew better than to interrupt him again.

'Anyway there's a small copse a couple of streets away from his home and he headed that way with me following. There was a bend along the pathway and he disappeared for a moment. As I turned the corner he'd stopped just ahead and was talking to a chap who was walking his dog. I needed to act fast or I would have been spotted so I jumped behind a hedge. I didn't realise there was a small stream running alongside. I slipped and fell in, picking up twigs and leaves along the way.' He heaved a big sigh. 'Luckily, he didn't see me.'

Megan noticed that his trousers were wet. He followed her gaze.

'Look, I'm going to go home and have a hot shower. I only came in to see if there were any messages.'

'Sorry, nothing. Even the phone hasn't rung.'

He looked a bit dejected at that comment. 'OK, I'd best be off. I need to get out of these muddy clothes.' He looked down at his clothes and shuddered. He looked at his watch. 'Not much point me coming back. Are you OK to lock up?'

'I'll be fine. See you in the morning,' she assured him.

He looked at her for a moment before inclining his head and walking out of the office shutting the door softly behind him.

Megan stood up and began picking up the stray leaves and twigs from the floor, smiling as she imagined Josh falling into the stream. Life certainly wasn't going to be boring working here.

4

A week later Josh was still grumpy. 'I'll catch him if it's the last thing I do,' he said as Megan put a cup of coffee in front of him. She'd just asked him how it was going with the Jimmy Donaldson case.

'I'm sure you will,' she said. 'I have every confidence in you.'

'You do?' He looked surprised. 'You hardly know me. I wouldn't have thought you'd have any opinion.'

'I'm trying to give a little encouragement here.' Honestly, the man was so touchy. 'Yeah, well thanks.' He took a sip of his coffee and returned his attention to a file on his desk.

'Anything interesting?' she asked, peering over his desk, trying to read upside down without much success as it only made her feel giddy.

'Just another case I'm working on. Wife suspects her husband of having an affair and needs proof for a divorce she

46

wants.' He tapped the folder. 'There's a lot of money involved and she wants her fair share. It should be easy to catch him but I can't be in two places at once. Unfortunately, Jimmy Donaldson seems to be taking up most of my time.'

Megan's eyes lit up. 'Maybe I can help. What do you need? A picture or a video of the husband getting up to no good?'

He shook his head. 'You've no experience plus you could get yourself into trouble, and I've got enough on my plate without that happening.' He rubbed the back of his neck in frustration then pushed back his chair and stood up. 'Look, I'm off out again. I got another tip-off this morning that Jimmy might be doing some gardening for a friend over the other side of town. It's my best hope of catching him to date.' He pulled on his jacket and pocketed his mobile phone. 'Text me if you need me. See you later.'

Megan watched him go. She wished she could help. It was obvious he was struggling to keep up with what work was outstanding.

She turned her attention back to the paperwork on her desk. Today she decided it was time to chase some outstanding debts. At least it would fill the bank account which might put a smile on Josh's face.

She'd just put the phone down on a customer who promised payment would be in the post that day when the phone rang again.'

'Hello, Merriweather and Rayne.'

'Is Mr Rayne there?' A woman's voice came down the line.

'I'm sorry, he's out of the office at the moment,' she told them. 'Megan Walters, his partner speaking. Can I help you?'

'It's Diane Swinson. Mr Rayne is trying to catch my husband out with that woman he's been seeing. Are you aware of my case?'

This was the client Josh mentioned earlier.

'Yes, of course, Mrs Swinson. I assure you Mr Rayne is working very hard on your behalf.'

'Not hard enough in my opinion. I expected results before now,' the woman grumbled.

Megan tried to apologise but the woman cut her off. 'Look, that's not why I called. I've been doing a bit of detective work myself and my husband will be at the Swan Hotel today. No doubt he won't be alone.'

'And you're sure about this?'

'As sure as I can be since the hotel rang to confirm the booking,' she said, dryly. 'Heaven help them when they realise they should have rung his office and not his home. Anyway, tell Mr Rayne to get down there and get the proof I need. From what I understand he's booked a table for two for lunch at one o'clock so he'll be able to catch them coming out about two-thirty. They thanked me for the booking and said they would see me later. He'll be there with that floozy of his.' There was a bitter note in the woman's voice and Megan could hardly blame her. 'Just tell Mr Rayne to get the job done. I expect results this time.'

Without further comment, the line disconnected leaving Megan staring at the handset.

She wondered what to do. Josh was busy with trying to catch Jimmy Donaldson. She should text him but would that help? Could he get to the Swan Hotel on time? She checked on google and found that the hotel was near the office. They couldn't afford to lose a client, which she was sure would happen if Josh didn't get the evidence today. It was only a picture that the woman needed. Megan could do that easily by using her mobile phone. She could even video it if needs be.

She recalled Josh's words that she wasn't to do anything stupid but this wasn't stupid, this was her chance to prove that she could be helpful apart from just doing clerical work. Wouldn't he be proud of her using her own initiative and managing to get the proof required?

She checked her watch. She needed to get moving if she was to arrive on time and find a decent spot to capture Mr Swinson and the floozy, as Mrs Swinson called her.

She went to Josh's desk and picked up the file he'd been talking about that morning. The name Swinson was printed on the front. She opened it up and there on the top was a picture of Mr Swinson, a tall man in his fifties with a thatch of greying hair. He wasn't bad looking and Megan could imagine why women were attracted to him. She popped the photograph into her handbag, switched the answerphone on, grabbed her bag and coat, locked up the office and headed off.

★ ★ ★

The hotel was set back off a quiet road with a circular driveway. It looked as though it would be difficult to find a good spot so as not to be seen but also get a good shot of the couple.

There were two pillars outside the hotel which stood either side of two huge doors, a wall ran along the side nearest

51

to her. Megan reckoned her best bet was to hide behind the wall and be hidden from sight by one of the pillars.

There was nobody about as she walked up the driveway and she crossed her fingers hoping that it would stay that way. She crouched down behind the wall, thanking her lucky stars that there were lattice designer bricks in the wall so she could see the comings and goings of guests from her vantage point. She would have to stand up to get a good picture but she was sure that she would be able to see Mr Swinson and his partner when they came out of the hotel.

She checked her watch — quarter past two. She wouldn't have long to wait. She pulled out her phone and put it onto silent. She didn't want to be disturbed. As she waited she watched a few people leave the hotel and some enter, none of them Mr Swinson. Her legs were beginning to feel like lead and she wanted to stand up and walk around before she got pins and needles.

Suddenly there he was, Mr Swinson

with a much younger woman on his arm emerging from the hotel. He pulled her towards him and she laughed at something he said before he bent down and kissed her.

Megan stood up and aimed her phone at the couple, snapping a picture as they locked lips. She must have made a noise because Mr Swinson turned round and caught sight of her.

'Hey, what do you think you are doing?' he said angrily. He walked towards her, his hand outstretched and tried to snatch her mobile from her hand.

'Hey, get off!' Megan shouted at him, quickly shoving the phone in her pocket before he could grab hold of it.

'I want that picture,' he said, his face getting redder by the minute. 'I don't like people taking pictures of me.'

Megan thought fast and put on her most indignant voice. 'I most certainly wasn't taking a picture of you. I was taking a picture of the architecture of the pillar. Exceptional work for the period. I'm a member of the local history group.'

She was talking rubbish but she doubted that Mr Swinson knew that. She watched him look at the pillar, then at her, doubt crossing his features.

She ploughed on, hoping her explanation would convince him. 'I'm sorry if you thought I was taking a picture of you, but you just walked into the shot as I snapped the picture. All perfectly innocent.'

'Oh, come on, Derek,' said the young woman. 'It was just an accident. No harm done.' She ran her bright red, manicured nails along the lapel of his jacket and gave him a beaming smile. His features seemed to soften and he smiled at the young lady.

Oh dear, thought Megan, *he's got it bad.* He glared at Megan. 'Just make sure you delete that picture,' he said, before taking the young women's arm and leading her away.

Megan stood and watched the couple walk towards the car park and gave a sigh of relief. What a lucky escape! She looked down at her phone and checked the image she'd just taken. It was perfect and all the proof Mrs Swinson needed. She watched as they got into a car and drove away out of sight before she made her way back to the office feeling pleased with herself.

* * *

Megan sat back in her chair silently clapping herself on the back. She'd helped with a case. Josh would be proud of her. But that wasn't how it turned out when an hour later he came storming into the office, anger flashing in his eyes.

'What on earth did you think you were doing?' he shouted at her as he walked into the office and loomed over her, his eyes deep black pools.

'What do you mean? I don't know what you are talking about,' she said, although she'd a pretty good idea exactly what he was talking about.'

'Mr Swinson,' he said, through gritted teeth. 'Mr Swinson?' Oh, heavens above, he looked furious.

'I've just received a call from a very angry Mrs Swinson. Apparently, he went home and mentioned that the architecture at the Swan Hotel was of interest to the local history group as a young woman was taking pictures of the frontage as he'd come out of the hotel after having lunch with a client and he'd accidentally had his photograph taken. She knew it was someone from this firm because she'd spoken to a Megan Walters earlier today. She expected a photograph to be taken discreetly, without her husband's knowledge. His suspecting anything could ruin her chances of a divorce.' He rubbed a hand across the back of him neck. 'Luckily Mr Swinson believed your tale about something to do with architecture, but my question still remains the same. What did you think you were doing? We spoke about you working outside the office only this morning.' His dark eyes pierced hers and she began to feel uncomfortable. 'Look, Megan, I appreciate you're now a partner in this business but your actions could have cost us a loss of business, which I might add, we can ill afford to do at the moment.'

'I'm sorry.' She felt like crying. She'd let him down and however much she wanted this partnership to work she could have jeopardised it by her own stupidity.

He looked at her for a few moments before sitting down at his own desk and taking a few deep breaths.

'Just don't do it again. If ever I need your help I'll ask you. OK?'

She said nothing for a moment, then pulled her mobile out of her handbag, pushing it over to him. 'Do you think you can use the picture?' She was pushing her luck but she felt she should try.

He scrolled through the directory until he came across her picture gallery with the picture of Mr Swinson and his girlfriend.

He studied it for a few moments. 'You did well,' he said, grudgingly. 'It should be just what our client is looking for. I'll talk to her.' He handed back the phone. 'Get a couple of copies printed off, one for the file and one for our client. Just promise me one thing.'

'What's that?'

'Don't ever do something like this without my knowledge again. I'm trying to increase business not lose it.'

'OK.' She turned back to the work on her desk sighing with relief. She said nothing else knowing that she'd got away with it but maybe next time she wouldn't be so lucky. If there was ever going to be a next time.

5

Sarah placed a cup of coffee and a plate of sandwiches in front of Megan. 'You don't look happy,' she said.

Megan had got into the habit of going into the café each day for lunch and over coffee and she'd become friendly with the café owner.

'Josh is still not speaking to me,' she admitted picking up her mug and taking a sip. She needed it. Trying to be pleasant to Josh was becoming more and more difficult. She'd told Sarah about the episode at the hotel, leaving out the names of the people involved obviously.

'He'll come round,' Sarah said. 'Just don't go upsetting him again. You know he's trying to make the business a success.' Sarah knew the family well, she'd gone to school with Josh and stayed friends over the years. 'He's worked hard, bringing in computers and trying to take on as much work as possible. His father was the same, the worker. Ronnie was a bit better when Josh's dad was alive because he didn't get away with much. It changed when Josh took over from his dad. He left more and more of the work to Josh.'

'Yes, I know. Josh explained it all to me. I was only trying to help.' She put her head in her hands and gave out a huge sigh. 'Perhaps I'm not cut out to do this kind of work. Maybe I should just hand everything over to Josh and let him pay me my share when he can afford it?'

Sarah reached out and squeezed her hand. 'Hey, don't give up. You like the work don't you?'

It was true she did like the job, it was so different from selling flowers and although she'd enjoyed her previous work this was a lot more challenging.

She gave a weak smile. 'You're right. I shouldn't give up. One slip up doesn't mean failure. I'll just have to try a bit harder. I just wish Josh would be on my side for once. Oh, I know he tries to be pleasant but sometimes I see it in his face.'

Sarah raised an eyebrow. 'His face?'

'Oh, you know a look that says *you shouldn't be here.*'

'Come on, eat up,' Sarah said, pushing the plate of sandwiches towards her. 'I think you need some brain food. All I can say is Josh is a good man and he'll come round in the end. It's just been a shock for him. Just imagine if you'd worked for years and expected a prize at the end, only to have it take away from you at the last hurdle.'

Put like that Megan could see where Josh was coming from. 'OK.' She bit into her sandwich and chewed. 'I'll see how it goes.'

'How about we go to the pictures tonight, cheer you up,' Sarah suggested. 'There's a new chick flick on at the local cinema I've wanted to see for ages, and I don't really fancy going on my own.'

Sarah was divorced and from what Megan could gather didn't have any intention of finding anyone else any time soon. 'Happy being independent,

61

owning my own business and living life just the way I want to,' she had told Megan. Reading between the lines Megan understood that Sarah's marriage wasn't a happy one and she was glad to get rid of her ex-husband.

'OK, that sounds like fun,' Megan said.

If she was honest with herself she was getting a bit fed up of just going to work and then home to a microwave meal for one and the TV. Too much of one's own company wasn't a good thing and she didn't want to brood about Josh and his attitude towards her.

'Be here at 7.00 o'clock. We can go for a late supper if you like. Make a night of it.'

Megan shrugged off her misery and smiled. 'Looking forward to it.' She finished off her lunch and stood up. 'I'd better go, just in case misery guts tells me I'm taking too long for lunch.'

'Hey, aren't you one of the bosses? You can have an extended lunch break.'

'I'll think about it when I make my

first million,' she said making Sarah laugh. 'See you later.'

★ ★ ★

She was just about to push the front door open to the office when it opened and a man in his fifties stepped out almost bumping into her.

'Sorry,' he said, stepping to one side and gesturing for her to enter.

A new customer she hoped, as he dipped his head and went on his way. Josh was studying a file in front of him when she walked into the office.

'Was that a new client I just saw leaving?' she asked, as she took off her coat.

He shook his head. 'No, another ongoing job'. He looked as though he was about to tell her more but was interrupted by a knock on the office door and it was pushed open. A woman in her thirties stood on the threshold, gripping a handbag. She looked nervous.

'Can we help?' Megan asked walking towards the woman.

63

'I'm not sure,' she said, biting down on her lip before taking a deep breath. 'I need you to find someone for me.'

Josh stood up then and put a smile on his face. 'That's what we're here for. Sit down and we'll see what we can do.' He ushered the woman towards a chair next to his desk and then turned to Megan. 'Put the kettle on would you, Megan.'

'Of course.' She gave the woman a wide smile hoping it would relax her. 'Tea or coffee?'

'Tea, no sugar,' the woman said.

As Megan busied herself Josh sat and pulled out a notepad and pen from his desk drawer.

'Now, how can we help you Mrs . . . ?'

'Oh, sorry. Mrs Frampton, Allison Frampton.'

'Nice to meet you, Mrs Frampton. I'm Josh Rayne and this is my partner, Megan Walters. Now, what's the problem?'

'It's my daughter.'

'You want us to find your daughter?'

The woman looked at him quite

alarmed. 'What? No! Oh dear, I'm not explaining myself very well am I?'

Josh leaned back in his chair and smiled at her. 'Just take your time.'

Megan handed her a cup of tea and sat down at her desk waiting for the woman to explain her visit. She was upset and her hand trembled as she took the cup from Megan. They both watched as she took a sip of tea and took a deep breath.

'My husband said it would be a waste of time but I told him that I just needed to try.' She looked first at Josh and then Megan. 'It's Lily, you see, my daughter. She's ill.'

Josh looked over at Megan and raised an eyebrow. What on earth has her daughter being ill got to do with finding someone?

'I'm sorry to hear that,' Josh said, sympathetically.

'Lily is ten and up until a few years ago was a happy, healthy little girl,' Allison Frampton went on to explain. There was a catch in her voice and Megan noticed that there was a tear forming in the corner of her eye.

'Take your time,' Megan said gently and received a grateful smile from the other woman.

'She started to get tired which wasn't like her at all. Always on the go, more like a tomboy than a little girl.' She smiled at the memory. 'I didn't take much notice at first just decided she was recovering from a bout of flu but she continued to feel low and in the end, I took her to the doctor. He took a blood test and then another and that's when we found out.'

Oh dear, this didn't sound good, Megan mused.

Allison hesitated as though she didn't want to say the next words. 'Lily has leukaemia and needs a bone marrow transplant.'

Josh was busy jotting down notes but stopped and frowned. 'I'm not sure how we can help Mrs Frampton, surely there is a donor bank that could be more helpful.'

'That's the problem. They can't find a match. It's been over a year and Lily is getting worse and worse.' She started crying and Megan handed over a box of tissues from her desk.

'Sorry,' she said, once her sobbing subsided.

'No need to be sorry,' Megan said. 'You must be at your wit's end.'

The woman sighed. 'My husband and I have been tested but we're not a match.'

'How about extended family?' Josh asked.

'We lucked out with Graham's family and there's only me on my side. My parents died some time ago. There's no one apart from Sheila.'

'Sheila?'

Yes, my Aunt Sheila. My mum's sister. She ran away years ago and nobody has seen her since. I was hoping she might be a match. She could save my little girl.' Allison Frampton started crying again and Megan got up from her desk and put an arm around her.

'It's going to be alright,' she said. 'We'll find her for you.'

She heard a cough and looked up to

see Josh shaking his head. Oh dear, she'd said the wrong thing again — but what else could she say to the poor woman who looked worn out with worry. She just glared back at him and patted the woman's shoulder.

Josh coughed again. 'We'll try our very best to find your aunt, Mrs Frampton. How about you give us as much information as you can?'

Allison Frampton went on to explain that Sheila and Allison's mother had argued over a boy. Sheila was seventeen and been dating the boy first but he decided her sister was a better option. Hurt and angry she ran away from home and apart from a postcard to her parents a few weeks later saying she was OK nobody ever heard from her again.

'My mother worried about it all her life and tried to find her. The argument over the boy was stupid and my mother only went out with him for a few months before it all fizzled out. How can someone just disappear like that?'

'Quite easily, I'm afraid,' Josh said as

he quickly made notes before looking up and giving the woman a wide smile. 'Now, how about we take down some information and then we can discuss how to proceed.'

'Her name is Sheila White and she'll be fifty-eight now.' She opened her handbag and brought out a photograph. 'This is her six months before she went missing. She'll have changed over the years but I don't have any other images of her.' She handed Megan the photograph. A young woman with long dark hair looked back. She stood next to another girl about a year older, Allison's mother she assumed. They must have been at a fairground as Megan could see a Ferris wheel in the background.

'Mum told me Sheila loved the fair and every year when it came to town they would go for the rides and the candy floss.'

Megan handed the photograph to Josh to study.

'I do have a couple of other things. Her diary. She left it behind, which was a surprise because Mum said that she wrote in it every night but she left in a hurry and forgot it I suppose.'

She pulled it out of her bag. It was one of those usual teenage diaries that girls liked so much with a lock on the front which wasn't working anymore. Her parents must have forced it open when their daughter disappeared. Megan flicked through it before passing it over to Josh.

'And then there's this.' Allison pulled out a postcard from her bag. It was tattered and the ends curled up but there was a clear picture on the front of a beach with a row of shops running along one side.

'As I said she sent this not long after she left home. Not sure it's much help but it's something.'

Megan took the postcard and looked at the writing on the back.

I'm OK. Don't try to find me. Sheila.

Short and sweet, not even a kiss for her parents but typical of a teenager who was only thinking of herself. She passed the postcard to Josh who studied it but said nothing.

'My grandparents went to the town where the postcard was posted from trying to find her but they didn't have any luck. They thought she'd come back once she'd calmed down but it never happened. They knew she was alright because of the postcard.'

'What about your mother? Did she ever try to find her?' Josh asked.

'A couple of times she put adverts in the national papers but it never came to anything. So do you think you can help? I know it's a long shot and she may not even be a match but I have to try, don't I?'

Josh dropped the postcard on his desk and looked at Allison. 'You most certainly do and as we've said we'll do our utmost to find your aunt but I must warn you that it might not be easy.'

Allison gave out a great sigh and smiled. 'Thank you, that's all I ask.'

'Good. Now, let's take down a few more details and then we can make a start.'

Half an hour later, Josh had all the

information he needed and shook the woman's hand.

'We'll be in touch, Mrs Frampton,' he said.

'Please call me Allison. I appreciate your help.'

'That's what we're here for,' he assured her.

Josh ushered the woman out of the office and shut the door before turning to Megan. 'I'm going to need your help with this one.'

Megan looked at him in shock. Did he say that he wanted her help?'

'Come on we need to get started. Everything else is on hold. A child's life is at stake'

Megan could only agree and they set to work.

* * *

'You seem much happier than you did this morning,' Sarah said. They decided to get a pizza and eat at Sarah's after the film.

Megan smiled. 'Josh has decided that my help is needed on a new case.'

Sarah's eyes widened. 'Oh, do tell,' she said, before biting down on a slice of pizza.

Megan lifted her fingers to her lips and motioned a sealed lips sign. 'Sorry. No can do. Client confidentiality.'

'Huh, and I thought I made a new friend who'd give me all the gossip.'

'I think you get enough gossip in the café.' Megan popped a piece of pizza into her mouth and chewed.

'True, but some of your cases must be so interesting.'

Megan wiped her mouth with a napkin. 'Not that I've noticed so far. Just the boring everyday stuff. You know, delivering paperwork to people who haven't paid their bills and such.'

Sarah looked thoughtful. 'Yeah. I suppose you're right. Oh well, maybe once this particular case is over you can disclose all the details.'

'Maybe.' Megan knew she wouldn't disclose any sensitive information. It wouldn't be fair on the client or the business.

She'd been quite happy after Allison's visit. She'd pulled up her chair next to Josh's and he'd gone through all the details of what was needed. They'd opened a file on the computer and added all the information they knew about Sheila White. Her age, date of birth and any other information they'd taken note of. There was very little there but at least it was a start.

'Pity her name is Sheila White,' Josh said.

'Why, what's wrong with her name?'

'Nothing apart from the fact that it's common. There must be thousands and thousands of women who have the same name.

'Mmm, I see what you mean. Perhaps if her name was,' she hesitated for a moment, 'Humperdinck, like that singer.'

Josh chuckled, showing his dimple and making Megan's stomach do a funny sort of flip. What was that all about?

'Do you know many people called Humperdinck?'

She tapped a finger to her lips, closing her eyes for a moment before opening then again. 'Now you come to mention it, I can't think of another.' Her eyes sparkled. They shared a laugh and the afternoon had quickly passed with both of them working in harmony.

Sarah clicked her fingers, bringing Megan back to the present.

'Must have been good, whatever you were thinking. You have a big smile on your face.'

Megan gave her a guilty look. 'Just thinking how nice it was working in a friendly atmosphere this afternoon. It's been a while since that happened.

'Told you things would look up. Josh isn't a bad bloke. Just got a bad deal in my opinion. Still, the outcome of Ronnie's will did have a good point.'

Megan raised an eyebrow. 'Oh, yes and what's that, then?'

Sarah nudged her in the ribs. 'I've found a new friend and you can never have too many of those.'

'That's true,' she agreed, giving Sarah a nudge in return and making them both laugh.

Megan wiped her hands on a napkin and pushed back her chair. 'Right, I think it's my bedtime. Josh seems to think we have a lot of work to do tomorrow.'

'Good luck with your detecting,' Sarah said as she stood on the doorstep of the café.

* * *

As Megan was unlocking her front door she noticed a man walking towards her. As he got closer she recognised Marcus, her ex. He looked as surprised to see her as she was.

'Megan, what on earth are you doing here?'

'Hello, Marcus. I could ask you the same question.' She kept her voice neutral remembering the angry words they'd said to each other the last time they met.

'Visiting a friend. You?'

'I've got a new job. Live over the shop so to speak.' She pointed to the doorway.

'Bit of a departure from selling flowers. What are you, the receptionist?' There was sarcasm in his voice which didn't surprise Megan. He'd never thought much of her job at the flower shop either.

'Would you believe a partner in the business?' she said with pride in her voice.

'Really?' He sounded surprised. 'Well, I must be off.' Without another word he walked past her, hurrying around the corner before she could say anything else.

Strange, he'd not asked her how she was or about the text she'd sent him finishing their relationship. Oh well, she doubted if she'd see him again so she dismissed him from her mind.

As Marcus turned the corner he pulled out his mobile and pressed the keypad. 'We need to meet. It's urgent. We have a problem.'

6

Megan felt a shiver of something as Josh placed a hand on her shoulder as he looked at her computer screen. They'd begun to work well together and Megan was beginning to like him more and more. She hoped that this case would be a turning point for both of them, particularly workwise. On the personal side she was finding herself becoming attracted to him, something she promised herself wouldn't happen after her last relationship went so badly. Concentrate on your career she told herself. 'Any luck?' Josh asked her. 'Nothing,' she said, trying to keep the disappointment out of her voice.

They'd spent the day searching different registers, electoral rolls and social media sites to see if they could find any information on Sheila White. So far all they'd discovered was that there were, as Josh predicted, an awful lot of Sheila

Whites in the country. It was an impossible task.

'At least we've found her birth certificate.'

It wasn't much help, only confirmed what they already knew.

'Coffee?' he asked.

'Please,' At the rate they'd been drinking the stuff she wouldn't sleep tonight.

'Don't look so dejected, we've only just started. We need to branch out, check other areas.' He placed a mug on her desk and walked back for his own.

'So far we've have nothing and hardly any other clues,' Megan said, taking a sip of the hot brew before returning her attention back to her screen. She took off her reading glasses and rubbed her sore eyes.

'Speaking of clues — we've got this.'

She looked over at Josh. He was holding the postcard in his hand. It was the last communication from Sheila.

'Pendry Cove, Devon,' Josh said, turning over the postcard and reading the small print. 'I think we should start there. I'll go tomorrow. See what I can find out.'

Megan bristled. So much for her thinking they'd turned a corner in their working relationship. She was not going to be stuck in the office while he was out following leads. 'I'm coming with you.'

He looked at her and sighed. 'We've been through this. You can't work on your own.'

'I won't be working on my own, will I? You'll be with me,' she said, reasonably. 'Just think of me as your sidekick. Anyway, two brains are better than one.'

'Who'll look after the office? Someone should be here.'

He was putting up obstacles. After beginning to feel they were getting on better he was blocking her again. It wasn't going to happen. She could be just as stubborn.

'How did you manage before me? The office was closed when you were out doing whatever it is you do.' She tried to keep the sarcasm out of her voice but it wasn't easy.

'I wasn't away for days,' he argued back.

'Do you think it will take days?'

He shrugged. 'I have no idea.'

'All the more reason why I can help. We can cover a larger area if there are two of us.

'I still don't think it's a good idea.'

He was being obstinate and she wasn't going to take anymore nonsense from him. 'Look Josh. I'm a partner in this firm, not just a clerical assistant. I do have some say it how this business operates.'

He opened his mouth to argue but she held up a hand. 'I'm coming with you and that's all there is to it. You can argue all you like, you won't win.'

He leant back in his chair and studied her for a moment. She was being as stubborn as himself and for some reason he admired that in her. Plus if he was honest he could do with the help and they did seem to work well together. He remembered the look on Allison Frampton's face when she spoke about her daughter.

They needed to find this woman quickly for little Lily's sake even if it didn't turn out the way her parents hoped.

He picked up the postcard and looked at the picture on the front and then flipped it over to read what was written on the back. He wasn't sure if they'd find out anything in Pendry Cove but it was worth a shot and time was of the essence.

He looked back at Megan. 'OK, you can come. We'll spend a couple of days there at the most and see what we can find out.' He looked at his watch. It was late and he'd promised his mother he'd take her out for a meal tonight. He pushed back his chair. 'I'm going to pack it in for the day and I suggest you do the same. Be ready for seven tomorrow morning. It's a long drive and I want to leave before the traffic gets heavy.'

He shrugged on his jacket and left without another word.

Well, it was a victory. He still hadn't forgiven her for the photograph episode. She'd show him though and helping to find the missing woman was just the opportunity she needed.

* * *

They made good time the next day. The traffic was light and the four hour journey seemed to pass quickly. They stopped on the motorway for something to eat and to discuss how they would start their enquiries. Megan hadn't a clue. Where did you start? There wasn't much on the postcard to give them a clue but when she mentioned this to Josh he shook his head, disagreeing with her.

'There's this,' he said, tapping his finger on the picture that lay on the table between them.

'What?' Megan asked, looking puzzled. She glanced at the picture again. A small half-moon beach with golden sands and a blue sea with white topped waves. Just a typical seaside postcard.

'There's a café,' he said, when he saw that she couldn't see what was right in front of her eyes. Megan peered closer.

Yes, she could see that, but how would it help? 'Happy Holiday Café. With any luck it will still be there. We have to start somewhere. Someone might remember her.'

'Bit of a long shot, don't you think? It's been over forty years.' Megan sounded doubtful.

'You'd be surprised how well people remember facts from the past. Trust me, Megan. I know what I'm doing.'

She inclined her head. She would have to trust him, wouldn't she? 'OK. Let's go.' She stood up wanting to get to their destination as soon as possible and find any clues that would help them in their quest.

★ ★ ★

Pendry Cove was a surprise. Megan was expecting to see what was on the postcard but over the years it had changed into a small town. Rows of white painted bungalows stood back a good distance from the cliffs looking down onto shops running along the seafront. They passed a large hotel a couple of miles outside of the town, newly built by the look of it.

'It's changed a lot,' Megan observed.

'The postcard was sent over forty years ago. It's progress,' Josh said as he manoeuvred the car onto the main street and towards the sea front. He found a parking spot and pulled in.

'We're in luck,' he said, pointing towards a building not far away.

Megan followed his gaze. It was the café from the postcard. It was updated a little, a fresh coat of paint but the sign read the same. Happy Holiday Café, nothing fancy, just told it as it was.

Josh stepped out of the car and stretched his legs removing the stiffness from his limbs after driving for such a long time. 'Come on, let's see what we can find out,' he said, walking towards the building.

The café was quiet. They were in luck that it was the end of season and most tourists were on their way home. A woman in her forties stood behind the counter and smiled as they walked towards her. 'Hi. What can I get you? Coffee, tea, a scone with cream and jam?'

Megan's mouth watered but Josh seemed impatient to find out what he could.

'We're looking for someone,' he said, after introducing themselves to the woman.

'Well, I know most people around here. What the name?'

'Sheila White.'

The woman frowned and thought for a moment. 'Sorry, I don't know anyone of that name.'

'She was here about forty years ago and sent her family this.' Josh handed over the postcard. 'Her family need to get in touch with her but haven't heard from her for a very long time.'

'Goodness, that's a long time ago!' the woman exclaimed and turned her attention to the postcard. 'This picture is ancient.'

'I know,' Josh said, taking the picture from the woman's hand and looking at it himself. 'Unfortunately it's the only clue we have. This is the last place the woman was when she made contact with her family.'

'Sorry, never seen her. I've been here over twenty years and I'd have remembered her if she lived around here.'

'So you weren't here in the late 70's early 80's?' Josh pressed.

'Sorry, no. Came here in the late 80's. Husband and I wanted a change of pace. Didn't mind being busy in the summer but needed to have the winters to ourselves. Now this lady, Sheila White — is she in any kind of trouble?'

'Oh, not at all,' Josh reassured the woman. 'It's just family issues.'

'Ooh, has she been left a load of money by a rich relative?' The woman seemed to be delighted at the idea.

Josh laughed along with the woman. 'You never know,' he said, winking at the woman.

He was putting on the charm, Megan realised. She liked his style. He was making the woman relax and hopefully offer up more information.

The woman pursed her lips and looked thoughtful. 'You know, maybe Joan Kendal could help you. She used to have the café before us. I mean she's elderly now but her mind is still as sharp as a tack.'

'That would be great. Does she live near here?'

The woman rested her hands on the counter. 'In one of those fancy bungalows overlooking the cove.' She bent down and reached for a notepad under the counter.

'Here's her address,' she said, scribbling on the pad before tearing the sheet off and handing to Josh.

'Thanks, I appreciate it.'

'Any time,' she said. 'Are you sure you don't want any refreshments?'

'Thanks, but no,' Megan spoke for the first time. 'But the scones look delicious, so we may be back. Thank you for all your help.'

'Hope you find who you're looking for,' the woman said and turned towards a couple who'd just walked into the café.

'Let's hope we get lucky,' Josh said when they got back to the car and drove to the address.

'Great view,' Megan observed as she stepped out of the car and turned towards the open sea. The day was sunny with only a few clouds in the sky. She could see a tanker out on the horizon and a couple of hardy sea lovers were surfing towards the beach. Josh was already walking up the path when she turned back and she hurriedly caught up with him.

'Maybe she's not in,' Megan said.

Josh rang the bell a second time. 'No, there's somebody coming. I see them through the glass.

A shadowy figure appeared behind the glass and they could hear the clicking of locks being opened. The door opened fraction and the face of an elderly lady appeared.

'You're the couple asking questions.' She said without waiting for Josh to explain who they were. 'Connie, the owner of the café just rung me.' She pulled the door open further. 'Come on in, I'll see if I can help you. No promises mind.' She shuffled her walking frame around and headed along the hallway

'Now what is it you want to know?' she asked, settling herself in a chair in her small lounge.

'We're looking for this woman.' Josh handed over the photograph. 'Sorry the picture isn't too clear. It was taken over forty years ago.'

Joan changed her glasses and looked at the picture.

'Her name is Sheila White. Her family want to get in touch,' Josh explained.

'Bit late after all these years,' Joan said, still studying the picture.

'She was a runaway. The police weren't interested because she was nearly eighteen. Almost an adult.'

Joan Kendal gave a wry smile. 'Don't we all think we're grown up at that age?' she muttered to herself.

Josh didn't comment. 'They received a postcard from her.' He handed over the postcard. 'Even came down here to search for her but they couldn't find her.'

Joan frowned. 'I don't remember them calling in at the café. Odd, because I do remember her. I have a good memory for faces.' She tapped the picture. 'She used to come into the café a lot, but her name wasn't Sheila. It was something else.'

'Really. Can you remember what?'

The old woman screwed up her eyes in concentration. 'It was Natalie as I recall,' she said after a moment.

Josh looked at Megan. 'She changed her name. No wonder we can't find any trace of her.' He turned back to Joan. 'Can you remember anything else about her?'

'She came looking for seasonal work. Found some shifts at the penny arcade on the sea front. As far as I can remember after that summer she left. Don't remember where she went. Nice girl though.' The old woman smiled. 'Used to make me laugh with all the jokes she knew.'

'So you have no clue where she went after that one summer?'

'Sorry no. There were a lot of young-

91

sters like that you know. Work the summer season to earn some money and then leave.'

Josh looked disappointed. It looked as though they'd reached a dead end. He stood up but halted with what Joan said next.

'Of course, you could ask Jerry Deaks, he might know.'

'Jerry Deaks?'

'Yes, he was her boyfriend that summer. Used to get on my nerves, all that kissing and cuddling over a couple of milk shakes that seemed to last forever. I used to tell them off. They put the tourists off coming into the café. He's still around here. Got his own fishing boat. Go back to the café and ask Connie. She'll know where you can find him.'

Thanking the woman, Josh and Megan left feeling a bit more positive.

'Clever, her changing her name like that,' Megan said as they settled themselves back into the car and headed back towards the café.

'I could kick myself for not thinking

of it. Of course if you want to disappear that would be one of the first things you'd do.'

'Back so soon?' Connie asked when they entered the café once more.

'Sorry to bother you again, but Joan does remember Sheila. She says she went out with somebody called Jerry Deaks and you would know where we could find him.'

'Oh, yes, I know Jerry but, you'll have to wait until tomorrow to speak to him.'

'Oh, really, why?' Josh looked disappointed.

'He'll be out fishing on that boat of his until the morning when he brings his catch in. He usually goes into The Jolly Fisherman after work. It's on the far side of the harbour. Easy enough to find.'

Megan realised they would have to spend the night. 'Do you know anywhere we can stay?'

'You are lucky it's the end of the season. Try Easterleigh Lodge, it's not far from the pub. They should be able to fix you up.'

'Come on let's find this boarding house.' He sounded excited and turned to her. 'It looks as though the chase is on.'

Megan couldn't help feeling the same excitement as she followed him towards the car.

7

They were in luck, there were plenty of rooms available at Easterleigh Lodge and they settled for the two at the front overlooking the cove.

It would be easy to watch the boats come in, Josh said, although Megan did point out that they didn't know what Jerry's boat was called. There was no way she was going to be up at the crack of dawn and check every vessel sailing into the harbour. She'd rather wait until after breakfast before they made further enquiries.

'You look more relaxed,' Megan said as they sat down for their evening meal. 'You're obviously pleased with what we've found out so far.'

He smiled and Megan tried not to think about how good looking he was with the worry lines easing from his forehead, his dimple appearing, and those warm brown eyes.

He took a sip of his wine. 'I just feel that we're on the right track to find Sheila, wherever she is. I'm just a lot more confident than I was twenty-four hours ago.'

Megan liked this relaxed Josh.

He cut into his meat and was thoughtful for a moment before looking at her, his dark eyes, bright with excitement. 'A few more jobs like this and I think we could be on the road to success. No disrespect to your family, Megan, but Ronnie was more of a hindrance than a help towards the end. Unreliable, never turning up for work. There was no way the business would have expanded with him in charge.'

'It must have been hard,' she said, understanding more of his reaction to her becoming his partner now. Hopefully, he would come to accept her in the weeks to come.

'I've been a little hard on you. I'm sorry about that but you must understand my position, I can't afford for anything to go wrong and this could be a big case for a small business like ours.'

She suppressed a smile He hadn't noticed how often in the last few minutes he referred to the business as 'ours' not 'his'. It must mean something — acceptance perhaps?

'So, you've never been asked to look for a missing person before?'

He shook his head. 'Not one.' He put down his knife and fork for a moment. 'But just imagine what it could do for us. Good publicity is never a bad thing.'

'Just remember that a child is sick in all this,' Megan pointed out. 'Her parents might not be happy with seeing their daughter's plight in the newspapers.'

His shoulders slumped a little. 'Yes, of course, you're right, but I'm sure they would think that it would highlight the problem of donor banks to help the sick.'

He made a good point. 'Perhaps you should mention it to Allison when you speak to her next.'

'I'll do that. Hopefully, she and her husband will think it's a good idea.'

They finished their meal and lingered

over coffee.

'How are you liking working in a detective agency?' Josh asked, spooning a couple of sugar cubes into his cup and giving the brew a good stir.

Megan chuckled. 'It's certainly different than putting bouquets of flowers together for customers. Although don't get me wrong, I did enjoy the work, but can I make a confession?'

She leant forward and whispered. 'This job is a lot more interesting.'

'As long as there are no more mishaps with photographs,' he said, reminding her of her first attempt at detecting. 'It took me ages to calm Diane Swinson down. Thankfully it turned out OK and when I gave her the proof she was happy to start proceedings against her husband. I think her last words to me were 'I'll take him for every penny he tells me he hasn't got.' He chuckled. 'I believe her.'

'Poor Mr Swinson. Sounds like he's in for a rough ride.' She looked serious for a moment. 'I am sorry, you know. I should never have gone off on my own like that, but I was just trying to help.'

He put his coffee cup down and looked at her. 'I know, but please, not again.'

She bit down on her lip before trying to stifle a yawn.

'Tired?' he asked.

'It's been a long day. I think I'll go to bed.' She pushed back her chair. 'See you in the morning.'

'Goodnight.'

He watched her walk out of the small dining room. He was beginning to like Megan, which was a dangerous thing. He'd no time for women at the moment. He needed to keep his focus on the main prize — the business.

★ ★ ★

It was too early to go to The Jolly Fisherman after breakfast so Josh suggested that they visit the arcade to see if there was anyone who remembered Sheila — or rather Natalie — all those years ago.

They packed their bags and Josh tossed them in the car. They wouldn't be returning.

The building was on one level with flashing lights enticing the public to enter as they approached from the roadside. The interior was nothing like how it would have looked in the late 1970s with the usual penny slot machines and the Space Invader games that were popular at the time. They'd been replaced with the latest video games — car chases, bullets flying from guns, and aliens trying to destroy different worlds.

Josh showed the picture of Sheila but nobody remembered her. Josh wasn't surprised as he explained to Megan.

'The majority of them weren't even born then, and a couple of the older guys in there are still not old enough to remember anyone who worked there during that time. Problem is we're going back a long way. This place has changed hands several times. Still, it was worth a shot just to see if we could jog someone's memory.'

Josh left them his business card anyway, just in case anyone remembered anything from all those years ago. They decided to call in at the café once more just to thank Connie for all her help.

Once again it was quiet, just a couple of women in the corner chatting about whatever over a cream cake and a coffee.

'We just wanted to thank you for all your help,' Josh said before ordering a couple of coffees to go. 'We're off in search of Jerry, now. Let's hope he can help us.'

'I hope so,' said Connie, crossing her fingers and holding them in the air before passing over their drinks.

Josh handed over some money. 'Can I give you this?' he said, pulling a business card out of his wallet. 'Just in case someone remembers anything. Joan promised to spread the word that we were looking for Sheila, or Natalie as she decided to call herself while she was here. 'We've assured Joan that the woman is not in any kind of trouble, just that her family would like to get in touch with her.'

Connie took the card from him and put in behind the counter. 'Well, if anyone tells me anything I'll let you know. Hopefully Jerry will be more forthcoming.'

'Do you think this ex-boyfriend will remember anything?' Megan asked as they took a slow walk towards the pub sipping their coffees.

'To be honest it's been a long time but it's amazing what memories people have,' Josh said as he walked alongside her. She'd been quiet all morning which was unusual for her.

'You OK?' he asked.

She shrugged. 'Fine. I suppose I imagined that we would get down here, find Sheila and report back to Allison. Job done.'

'If only it was that easy,' Josh sighed. 'Detective work is a lot harder than that. Look how long I've been trying to catch Jimmy Donaldson. To be honest I'm happy with what we've found out so far. I thought it would take much longer than this.'

'But what have we found out?

He held up his hand and began counting off his fingers. One, Sheila stayed here for the summer. Two, she changed her name to Natalie. Three, she went out with a chap called Jerry who we are now going to interview to see what he remembers. That's three things we didn't know before.'

'I suppose so,' Megan said, 'But it still doesn't help me thinking that we could have wrapped this up much quicker.'

He stopped walking, causing her to stop and look at him. 'And why did you think that? Maybe I have a magic wand in my desk and I waved it about and all of sudden the woman would appear?'

He sounded irritated and she couldn't blame him. 'Sorry,' she said, feeling ashamed. 'Just me being stupid. Of course, we should be more positive. I have a lot to learn, don't I?'

His face softened and much to her surprise smiled his dimple appearing. 'Come on let's see if we can get the fourth bit of information on our list.' He took hold of her hand and gave it a squeeze. It was warm and felt as though it should be there. She was a little disappointed when Josh let go and carried on walking.

★ ★ ★

Jerry Deakes was not what Megan imagined at all. The years hadn't been kind to him. His weathered face was leathered with age, his skin conker brown from the sun and the salt of the sea. He wore a heavy coat and a woollen cap on his head, He nursed a pint of beer as he sat at the bar. Fishing was hard work and he appeared tired after bringing home his catch.

'Mr Deakes?' Josh said after the landlord pointed him out to the couple.

'That's me,' he said, taking a gulp of beer from the glass in his hand. 'You that couple who've been looking for me?'

Megan looked surprised but she noticed Josh kept his face impassive.

'You've heard about us then?' he said, calmly.

'News travels fast around here.'

'So you know we want information about Sheila White, or Natalie as you would have known her.'

He gave a chuckle. 'Oh, I knew what her real name was. Told me all about herself when we started dating. Hated her given name. Fancied herself on the silver screen. Liked that film star, Natalie Wood so decided that was what she was going to be called from then on.'

'Can you tell us a little bit more about her?'

Jerry Deakes drained the rest of his pint. 'Cost you,' he said, brazenly pushing his empty glass towards Josh.

Megan watched as Josh didn't bat an eyelid but just gestured to the barman to refill the fisherman's glass. He ordered a half for himself and raised an eyebrow at Megan.

'Nothing for me, thanks,' she said.

Josh looked over at some empty seats in the corner and once their drinks were poured suggested they go and sit down for some privacy. Jerry picked up his pint and followed them.

'So, what can you tell us?' Josh said as they settled down.

'What do you want to know?'

'Everything.'

Jerry took a long pull of his pint and leant back in his seat.

'I was nineteen when I met Natalie. First off she was just a girl who came down for the summer to work the holiday season. She was working in the arcade when I first saw her. Pretty little thing.' He smiled in remembrance. 'Anyway, she must have seen something in me because I asked her out and she agreed. I must say we had quite a summer.' He wiggled his eyebrows suggestively and winked. 'I wanted her to stay, you know. Planned on asking her to marry me, but she would have none of it. Made plans, she said. Marriage wasn't included. I can tell you I was disappointed I really did think we made a great couple, but you can't hold on to something that was never there in the first place, and Natalie was a bit like a bird, needed to fly away when winter closed in.'

'Any idea where she went?' Josh asked.

'She never said. Just disappeared one day without a word. Haven't heard from her since. Just flew away.' He raised his hand and did a flying motion with his fingers before taking another sip of his pint. 'Sorry, can't help you anymore. To be honest, it was so long ago and I've moved on since.' He finished his pint and stood up. 'Must be off. The wife is waiting for me. A local girl with no intention of leaving the nest. Going to see the grandkids today.'

'Thanks for all your help,' Josh said, shaking the man's hand and offering him his card. 'If you do remember anything at all could you give me a call? It's very important to her family. They're desperate to get in touch.'

Jerry looked at the card and tucked it into his jacket pocket. 'Will do.'

Josh drained his glass of beer and they said their goodbyes outside the pub.

They'd learnt a lot more about Sheila but as to finding her — they were no further forward.

8

Megan pushed her chair back in frustration. She'd spent all day going through search engines, social media sites and any other forms of information she could think of and still she couldn't find the elusive Sheila/Natalie White.

She pulled out a bar of chocolate from her desk drawer. Comfort food was just what she needed. She broke off a huge chunk and popped it into her mouth, closing her eyes in sheer delight as the sweet, velvet taste coated her tongue.

They'd been back a day and Josh left her to do the searches while he, yet again, went out trying to catch Jimmy. At least he was persistent. She would have given up ages ago. The guy was just too clever for his own good.

She picked up Sheila White's folder to see if there was anything she'd missed and the diary that Allison gave them fell out. They'd both taken a curious glance at it when they were given it but hadn't paid much attention to a teenager's musings which, if she was honest, was a bit remiss of them. There must be a clue hidden between the pages . . .

Monday 8th — Linda's been out with him again, gorgeous Martin. Why did she have to set her sights on him? I saw him first. He smiled at me first. He was mine first. I hate her!

Oh dear, Sheila certainly didn't like her sister!

Wednesday 10th — Linda's going out with Martin again. She's even bought a new top. Bet she'll flutter her lashes at him and he'll be in love. He's mine, always has been and I'm going to get him to pay attention to me. Just you wait!

Friday 12th —Went to see Julie and Anne. My best friends said they are going to back me all the way and we thought of all sorts of evil things to do to Linda. A laxative in her drink is the best we can come up with. Will stop her going out with Martin!

Sunday 14th — Laxative didn't work. Had a big row with Linda.

There were no other entries. Megan could read between the lines that Sheila was very unhappy. It was clear that Sheila and Linda didn't get along and the issue with the boyfriend was causing a big rift between the two of them,

On the plus side, there were a couple of leads in the diary that she could work on. She could've kicked herself for not reading the diary earlier but they were both so positive that going with the lead of the postcard would get results.

She picked up the phone and dialled.

'Hi, Allison, Megan Walters here.'

'Have you found her?' There was hope in the woman's voice and Megan felt awful having to disappoint her.

'Sorry, no but we do have a few leads,' she said on a positive note.

'Oh, right. Well, what can I do for you?'

'I'm reading Sheila's diary and she mentions a few people. Someone called Martin and her best friends, Julie and Anne. Any idea who they are?'

'Oh yes, Martin Coles, the boy they fell out about and Julie and Anne Nelson,

111

they're twins and were her best friends. They all still live around here.'

'Oh, that's great. I don't suppose you have their addresses to you?'

'I might have the twins address in one of Mum's old address books. Not sure about Martin Coles.

I only know he still lives around here because Mum pointed him out to me once and I see him occasionally.'

'If you could get me their address as soon as possible that would be great. They might know something. I'll track down the boyfriend myself.'

'I know that my grandparents asked the twins if they knew anything at the time and they claimed they hadn't a clue. Not sure if they spoke to Martin.'

'No worries, we'll see what we can find out.' Megan paused for a moment. 'How's Lily?'

'Holding up, but still no donor.' There was a catch in Allison's voice and Megan could almost feel the woman's pain.

She wished they'd decided to do some publicity to help the search along, but when Josh mentioned it both parents declined, wanting to keep the matter private.

'Sorry, I didn't mean to upset you.'

'You didn't. I just wish that something would happen. All this waiting is a strain on my nerves.'

'I'm sure it is,' Megan said, sympathising with the woman. 'Just hold on and hopefully we'll find your aunt.' She tried to put a positive note in her voice. Allison Frampton needed something to hold onto at the moment.

'I appreciate all you're doing, Megan. I know it's a long shot and nothing may come of it but I have to try.'

'Of course you do. I'll speak to you as soon as I have any further information.'

'OK. I'll go and search out that address and email it to you.'

'That'll be great.' Saying goodbye she put the phone down and leant back in her chair. Josh would be pleased that she'd managed to get some more information.

It was late when he arrived back and

he didn't look at all happy.

'Another bad day with Jimmy?' she asked, not looking him in the eye.

He flopped down in his chair and ran a hand through his hair before giving out a big sigh in frustration. 'You know it's almost as if he knows I'm watching him. He has this inner ability to know I'm there. I'm not sure how he does, but at the moment he's beating me at this cat and mouse game.'

'Perhaps you should lay off him for a little while,' she suggested. 'Maybe giving it a rest for a short time will relax his guard.'

Josh looked at her or a moment. 'You know that's not a bad idea. I might just do that. Good suggestion.'

Megan looked over at him and smiled, at least she'd made a good suggestion. She picked up the diary from her desk and waved it at him.

'I've been doing some digging while you were out. Read some of Sheila's entries in her diary.'

'Anything interesting?'

She tapped the diary. 'There were a couple of friends plus the chap her and her sister were fighting about, Martin is his name. So I rang Allison Frampton who told me she has the address for the friends but not his. She sent the information that she has, plus a phone number.' She waved a piece of paper. 'We are going to interview Sheila's friends tomorrow morning. Twins, Julie and Anne Nelson. I'm still trying to find out more information on the boyfriend, Martin Coles.'

He stood up and moved around his desk. 'Well done,' he said, giving her a hug. 'We'll make a detective out of you yet.'

Megan blushed bright red and untangled herself from Josh. She quite liked the warmth of his body against hers and the smell of his woodsy aftershave. For a moment she was quite disturbed by the effect he was having on her. Of course, it was just a gesture in the heat of the moment, he meant nothing by it. She went back to her desk and began logging out of her computer.

'I think I'll finish for the day. I've been invited to Sarah's for a meal.'

'OK. Say hi from me. I haven't seen her for a while. Tell her I'll call in for a coffee soon,'he said, picking up the diary from her desk and flipping through the pages. 'Have a good evening.' He held up the diary. 'I think I'll see if I can find out any more information from this and we'll go over anything else in the morning.

The phone rang. 'Merriweather and Rayne, how can I help you?' said Megan. She listened for a moment before putting the call on hold. ' Mr Blackstone from Blackstone Construction.'

'Ah, thanks, I've been expecting his call.'

She raised an eyebrow. 'New customer?'

He shook his head. 'No, but the case is on hold for the moment. I'll explain later. You go off and enjoy your evening.'

She wanted to stop and ask him what the case was all about. Marcus, her ex worked for Blackstone Construction.

Was there a problem with the business? Probably not, more like it was something personal that Mr Blackstone required investigating. She was running late so decided to ask Josh in the morning.

★ ★ ★

Megan pushed her plate away and gave a big sigh. 'Wish I could cook like that,' she said. 'That spaghetti bolognaise was perfection.' She touched her fingers to her lips in a kissing motion. 'I don't know why you don't serve more home-made food in the café. You'd be packed every day.'

Sarah shook her head. 'And end up with a headache every day. No thanks. I'm happy with the clientele I have already.'

'So, you're not interested in making a fortune and retiring early?'

Her friend laughed. 'I earn enough to keep me comfortable and with no pressure. My customers are great and to be honest, I like my life just the way it is.'

117

'You never get lonely then?'

Sarah stood up ignoring the question and began clearing away the plates.

'Hey,' Megan protested. 'You cooked, I'll wash up.'

'You're a guest, and anyway it only takes a minute to pop these dishes in the dishwasher.' She disappeared into the kitchen with Megan following her.

'At least let me make the coffee.'

'It's all yours,' Sarah said pointing the coffee machine on the worktop.

As she busied herself making the brew she looked over her shoulder at her friend. 'So are you trying to avoid my question?'

'What question?' Sarah avoided Megan's eyes.

'Being lonely.'

'No, never, and if you're asking if I want a man in my life the answer is no, not at the moment.'

'I feel as though there's a 'but' in there somewhere.'

Sarah shrugged and turned on the dishwasher. 'There may come a time when I might consider finding someone, but as I said, not at the moment. 'What about you?'

'Me?'

'Is there a man in your life?'

Megan was reminded of Marcus. She hadn't mentioned him to Sarah preferring to forget about him. 'Not currently, no.'

'I'm surprised, good looking young woman like you. I was sure they'd be queuing up for a date.'

'Thanks for the good looking bit.' She didn't think of herself as good looking, just ordinary. OK, her shoulder-length hair was thick and dark, but she did have a tendency to blush at the slightest thing. She put her coffee mug on the small table in front of her. 'Like you, I'm quite happy in my own company.'

'What about Josh?'

'Oh, I don't think he's got a girlfriend.' Megan knew what her friend was asking and deliberately tried to misdirect her.

Sarah studied her over the mug. 'You know exactly what I mean.'

'If you're asking if Josh and I are interested in each other, the answer is no. Josh doesn't look at me in that light at all. To him, I'm just a nuisance that was willed to him when Great Uncle Ronald died. I'm sure if he could he would get rid of me tomorrow.'

'Hmm.'

'What is that supposed to mean?'

'I think you protest too much.'

Megan looked across at her friend, shocked by what she said. 'What on earth makes you say that? I can honestly say that I have no interested in Josh whatsoever.'

'So how come you've spent most of the evening talking about him, then?' Sarah asked.

'I have not,' she protested but felt a blush rising on her cheeks.

'Really?' Sarah said. 'Josh is getting used to me in the office. Josh is such a good driver. Josh and I went down to Devon on a case. Josh asks some really good questions.' She ticked the items off on her fingers.

'You asked me where we went. I just mentioned that Josh and I were away on a case but I can't talk about it. And to be fair he is a good driver. But I can assure you I have no interest in him in a romantic way. We're just business partners. That's all. Can we change the subject?'

She reached for her coffee cup and bent her head, her dark hair falling around her face to hide the heat in her cheeks.

She wasn't quite sure why she felt so flustered over Sarah's interrogation of her relationship with Josh, or rather lack of any relationship. She liked him even though she knew he would rather have the business to himself, and to be fair they were getting on a lot better over the last few weeks. He'd complimented on her getting all the invoices out and collecting money owed. In fact the bank balance for the business was starting to look quite healthy. He did, however, want to increase the business. Even told her that to sustain both of them with a comfortable living the turnover needed to be higher.

'How about I take you out for a meal next time? I'd offer to cook but I'm not sure you'd welcome beans on toast even if it's served to you on a silver platter!'

Sarah chuckled. 'I'm sure you're not that bad. I could always show you a few simple recipes if you like.' She raised an eyebrow. 'Just in case you ever want to entertain a gentleman friend.'

Megan pulled the cushion from behind her back and threw it in Sarah's direction. 'Stop it! No more talk of men.'

Both women laughed.

'How about I find some easy recipes? You can come round here in a couple of days and I can see how you do slaving over a hot stove.'

'Sounds appealing,' said Megan, laughing. 'But don't blame me if I set the kitchen on fire.'

'Not a chance. I'll keep an eye on you. Plus I don't believe you're as bad as you say.'

'You could always ring my mother.

She'll tell you how bad I really am. The only thing I'm allowed to do at her house is wash-up, and even then I have to be supervised.'

Sarah put her hands in the air. 'OK, I believe you, but I plan on changing things. By the time I've finished with you, you'll be a good cook.'

Megan shuddered. 'Good luck with that.' She yawned. 'I think it about time I headed home. It's been a great evening, thanks for inviting me.' She shrugged on her coat and picked up her handbag. 'I'll see you tomorrow.'

★ ★ ★

Getting ready for bed Megan's thoughts returned to the conversation with Sarah. Did she really talk so much about Josh, and if she did, why?

The answer would come in the weeks ahead.

9

Julie and Anne Nelson were nothing like Megan imagined, although if she was honest she wasn't sure what she expected. Anne wore her long dark hair in a bun, Julie's short blond hair was styled in a bob. One thing was for sure, they both wore great big smiles of welcome when they opened the door the next morning.

'Come in, come in,' they both beckoned.

The small terraced house was as neat as a pin and Megan and Josh followed the twins into a small living room.

'We've made cake. Cup of tea?' Julie asked, after gesturing for them to sit down. 'Lemon drizzle or jam sponge?' Without waiting for an answer she cut into the sponge, Anne doing the same with the lemon drizzle. Tea was poured into dainty, china cups.

Megan held back a chuckle as she watched Josh try to pick up the cup with his large hands, in the end giving up and leaving it to go cold.

'This is so exciting,' said Julie. 'Nothing much happens to us, you know. We both work at the local council so apart from going to work and coming back nobody ever visits, although we do go out once a week, a tea dance on a Sunday.'

Megan was surprised. They didn't seem the type to be friendly with the outgoing Sheila.

Anne rested a hand on her sister's arm to halt her talking. 'I think they want to talk about Sheila not listen to what we get up to.'

'Oh, yes, I forgot. What can we tell you? It was such a long time ago.' She threw a glance at her sister. 'Poor Sheila, I wonder where she is now?'

Anne squeezed her sister's hand. 'Very upsetting when she went off like that.'

'Her family are looking for her,' Megan said. 'We wondered if *you* had any idea where she is.'

Julie looked at Anne before they both

looked across at Josh and Megan. 'Not a clue. Sorry,' they said in unison.

'What was she like?' Josh asked.

'Oh, she was so much fun, always getting into mischief,' Anne said.

'We were such close friends from junior school onwards. She was always the one leading us into mischief,' Julie said, before turning to her sister. 'Do you remember when we played truant? It was so daring in those days. There was some film or other on at the local cinema that we all wanted to see but it was too adult in the opinion of our parents. Anyway Sheila would have none of it and we all made up some excuse to get out of school for the afternoon.'

Anne laughed. 'Oh, yes that's right. We said we had a dental appointment. Our teacher didn't suspect a thing since we were twins and did most things together. I can't remember how Sheila got out of lessons but I remember we all met up and went to the pictures and never ever got caught. Sheila loved the cinema. Always considered herself a bit of an actress. She was leading lady in a couple of the end of terms plays and declared she was going to be in films when she grew older.'

Julie giggled. 'She didn't manage it, did she? I mean she couldn't have because I've never seen her on TV. Although she always wanted to change the colour of her hair. Decided she would look more glamorous if she was blond rather than the dirty brown as she referred to her hair.'

'I rather liked her hair,' Anne said, 'Not dirty at all, a rich brown colour. To be honest I was quite envious.' She patted her own thinning hair.

'So do you think she might have gone to London?' Megan asked. It was all very well that the ladies reminisced about days gone by, it was all very helpful information, but they needed to know a bit more.

The twins looked at each other for a moment, something Megan noticed they did a lot during the conversation. They seemed to have some sort of telepathy going on and a silent question and answer routine between them before answering.

'She could have, but we never heard from her, so wouldn't know.'

'Why do you think she left? We know there was some sort of row with her sister but that seems a bit of a drastic action to take. After all sisters do argue, don't they?'

'We don't,' said both sisters, shaking their heads and looking surprised at the suggestion.

No, Megan couldn't imagine they ever did. 'That's good, but Sheila and her sister Linda did frequently, didn't they?'

Both ladies gave a big sigh and looked at each other. 'Yes, they did,' admitted Anne. 'You have to understand that Sheila always felt she wasn't good enough. Linda was the clever one. The one their parents were most proud of. The one that never got into trouble.'

Julie took over. 'It wasn't true, of course, but Sheila believed it, which was all that really mattered. Then, of course there was Martin.' She fidgeted in her seat before looking at her sister who inclined her head. 'Martin Coles was the hottest boy around and Sheila started to go out with him. She fancied herself in love. It was silly nonsense really and we used to laugh about it didn't we, Anne?'

'Not in front of Sheila, of course, that would have been cruel,' Anne hastened to add.

'Anyway,' Julie continued, 'They'd been going out for about a month and Sheila began to gaze at engagement rings. She talked about Martin becoming her manager when she became famous and they'd live in a big house and she'd have a break from the stage and have a couple of children. She even said we could be bridesmaids at her wedding.'

The twins laughed at the idea. 'They were such happy times,' said Anne. 'Of course, it didn't happen that way because once Martin laid eyes on Linda it was all over. Poor Sheila was distraught. Can you imagine finding the love of your life and then losing him to your sister who, in your eyes, always got everything she wanted?

Megan could almost feel sorry for poor Sheila whose happiness was snatched away from her in a moment. She recalled the poster of the pop star on her childhood bedroom wall. How she cried when she found out he was getting married! Young love was harsh.

'What happened to Martin Coles?' asked Josh who'd been quiet for most of the conversation. He just sat there with a notepad resting on his lap taking notes as the ladies told their tale.

'Oh, he still lives around here,' Anne said. 'On the council estate just outside of town with his wife. We see him about sometimes don't we Julie?'

Her sister agreed. 'He might have heard from Sheila, although I doubt it. They argued before she left home. He was quite cruel really. Laughed at her when she told him that she loved him.'

'More tea?' Anne asked, picking up the teapot.

Josh covered his still full cup with his hand. 'No, thanks. We must be going.

You've been very helpful, thank you.'

'We hope you find her. Is it some sort of family reunion? Is that why you're looking for her?

Josh stood up. 'Something like that.' He pulled a business card from his pocket and handed it to Julie. 'If you think of anything else, let us know.'

'Of course, anything to help,' the twins said together before waving them off.

'So what do you think?' Megan asked as she settled herself into the car.

'Some useful information. They certainly knew Sheila very well and about the jealousy between the two sisters.' Josh frowned.

'What's wrong?'

He sighed deeply. 'I don't know. It's just that something just doesn't feel quite right. I mean, if they were such good friends why didn't Sheila tell them where she was going? Surely she would have confided in them. That's what you do, don't you? Being best friends you'd need someone to talk to. Would you really go off just like that?'

'Perhaps she decided they would say something. It's difficult to keep secrets when you're teenagers. You like to gossip, don't you?'

He gave her a long look. 'I suppose so.' He turned the key and the engine roared into life. 'Right, back to the office, then — we have some work to do.'

★ ★ ★

The next couple of hours was spent with Megan updating the information they'd received from the twins onto the computer while Josh traced where Martin Coles lived and made arrangements to see him that afternoon.

'Fancy something to eat?' Josh asked after he spoke to Martin Coles. 'We can grab something from Sarah's before going to our appointment.'

Josh was beginning to include her more and more which pleased Megan. 'Good idea. I'm becoming quite addicted to her ham and cheese Paninis.' She grabbed her coat and followed him out of the office.

The café was busy with the lunchtime rush but they managed to find a table at the back.

'Be with you in a minute,' Sarah called as she busied herself serving a group of workers.

'Do you think we're getting any closer to finding Sheila?' Megan asked.

Josh scrubbed a hand across his jaw and looked thoughtful. 'I'm not sure but every piece of information we uncover brings us closer to getting a result. We just have to be patient. Just like I am with Jimmy Donaldson. He's got the upper hand at the moment, but I'll catch him in the end.'

There was a steely note in his voice and Megan didn't doubt for a moment that he would succeed.

Megan reached out and touched his hand. 'I have absolute faith in you.'

He looked down at her hand. She felt herself blush and quickly removed it. 'What do you fancy to eat?' she said to cover the awkwardness.

'Just coffee and a sandwich,' he said, seemingly happy to move the conversation on.

She was about to stand up and go to the counter when Sarah arrived at their table.

'Hi Josh, long time no see.'

'Been busy, Sarah.' He looked around the café. 'Business looks good.'

'Can't complain. How's yours? Got a new partner, I see.' She smiled down at Megan.

'I have and I gather she's been keeping you in business for the last few weeks.'

'Hey, this lady has to eat,' Megan said, laughing as she joined in their banter.

Once Sarah had jotted down their order and disappeared, Megan said to Josh, 'She's a good friend to you?'

'She is. I've known her since junior school.'

'Bet she has some tales to tell.'

Josh grimaced. 'I'm sure she has but not some that I'd like repeated.'

Megan raised an eyebrow. 'Really? Now you have me intrigued. What could you possibly have got up to as a school-boy that you wouldn't want me to know?'

Josh tapped his nose and there was a twinkle in his eye. 'Nothing that I care to reveal.'

'What doesn't she need to know?' Sarah appeared with their food and pulled up a chair. 'The lunchtime rush is slowing and Stacey appears to be coping. I have time for a chat. So come on, what's to know.'

Josh groaned. 'Nothing.'

Megan laughed and decided not to let Josh off the hook. 'He was just saying that you know all his secrets from when you were at school together. Care to share?'

Sarah dropped her hands on the table and leant towards Megan. 'Oh, I most certainly do,' she said, winking at Megan causing them both to laugh and Josh to groan even louder.

'How about I start with Suzie Hadfield and a certain kiss.'

Megan looked over at Josh who was now looking extremely uncomfortable.

'Kissing the girls at school, Josh. Did

135

you get caught?'

'He most certainly did, and by Mrs Baily, the headmistress, no less.'

'Tell it like it is, Sarah,' Josh grumbled. 'You might like to mention that I was only seven years old and that Mark Oldham dared me to do it.'

Megan burst out laughing with Sarah joining in.

'He was a proper Casanova at that age!' Sarah said, trying to control her laughing.

'Is he still?' Megan asked, then wondered why she'd asked the question. He was an attractive man and she wondered if he was in a relationship. He'd never mentioned anyone special although their conversations were never that intimate.

'I'm not sure. I haven't seen him with anyone for a while.'

'Hey, I'm sitting right here,' Josh said. 'How about you, Megan — anyone special in your life?'

He hadn't answered the question, just turned the tables on her. She was quiet for a moment before realising that both Josh and Sarah were looking at her expecting an answer.

'No one at the moment. My last relationship ended a few months ago.' She didn't elaborate. There was no need to mention Marcus.

'It looks like the two of you are single and fancy free. Maybe you should get together.' Sarah winked. She was only teasing but they both looked uncomfortable.

'Shut up, Sarah,' Josh said giving her a stern look. He picked up his sandwich and began eating and the conversation ended.

'I think I'd better get back to work,' Sarah said sensing that she'd over stepped the mark.

Josh grunted but said nothing further.

'I'll chat to you later,' Megan said to her friend before turning back to her own food, not sure what to say now.

Josh sat chewing his food. He never asked Megan about her love life but somehow he was pleased that she didn't have a boyfriend. He wondered about her last relationship, although for the life of him he couldn't think why it would interest him. He drained his cup of coffee and checked his watch. 'It's time we went to meet Martin Coles.'

Megan pushed back her chair and grabbed her coat. 'Let's hope he can give us some more information.'

She seemed to be relieved that the conversation turned back to work, thought Josh as he followed her out onto the street. Once again he wondered what the story was about her love life and why he was so interested. He shook his head to remove any idea of romance and turned his mind to the interview ahead.

10

Martin Coles was no longer the hottie Sheila White fell in love with all those years ago. His dark hair was thinning and he had a comb-over, which never worked on any man in Megan's opinion. His waistline also hadn't been kind to him and now expanded over the top of his trousers.

'Jane, put the kettle on, love,' he said to his wife as he gestured for them to sit down. A pleasant-looking woman smiled at them and disappeared into the kitchen. 'Lucky you came today. Since I took early retirement, the wife and I spend most of our time doing all the things we were never able to do while we were working.'

He chuckled. 'Although I haven't taken up sky diving as yet. Mostly fishing and a bit of golf, plus the wife likes us to take the grandchildren out as much as possible.'

He settled his large frame in an old overstuffed chair which Megan assumed was his favourite by the way it sagged as he sat down.

'Now what can I do for you? I must admit I'm curious when you mentioned Sheila White, now that's a name from the past. Way back in my youth. When I was young, handsome and slim.' He patted his stomach. 'Good times are long gone.' He was silent for a moment most likely thinking about those good old days.

His wife came back with a tray of tea and Josh waited until she settled down in a chair next to her husband.

'You know Sheila disappeared,' Josh said, 'Or rather, ran away, and has not been heard of since. Her family are looking for her.' He turned to Martin's wife. 'I hope you don't mind me talking about Martin's old girlfriends?'

Jane laughed. 'Not at all. He confessed all his crimes before we got married. Did he tell you he was quite a looker in his day? All the girls chased him.' She leaned over and nudged Martin. 'Pity he's partial to steak and kidney pudding with mashed potatoes.'

'But you love me just the way I am,' Martin said, rubbing his expanding stomach.

'Anyway, back to Sheila White and her running off,' Josh said returning the conversation back to the matter in hand. They were a nice couple but Josh wanted to get as much information out of the man as possible without distractions.

Martin folded his arms across his ample chest. 'Yes, I knew that she'd run off. I used to go out with her, but not for long, much referred Linda. She wasn't so clingy. Just wanted to have a good time. Sheila was different. Do you know she wanted to get married?' He laughed and shuddered at the same time. 'Not for me. I was too young, wanted to see a bit of life before I settled down. Plus I didn't always believe what she said. You know, about the settling down. She'd some idea in her head that we'd go off to London and become an actress and I'd be her manager. Now, how daft is that?'

He took a long breath and looked into the distance before he spoke again.

'Of course, once I met Linda things were a lot different. I suppose if I was older I would have done things differently but when you're young and consider you're the bee's knees you think you can get away with anything.'

He looked over at Josh who said nothing and Megan wondered if Josh would ever treat a girl badly. Somehow she didn't think so.

'Anyway,' Martin continued, 'I was a hot-blooded young male in those days. For some reason, the girls liked my handsome face and dark curly hair. 'He touched the top of his head. 'Shame about the curls, lost them in my late twenties. Not a lot left now. Anyway Linda seemed to like me and at first, she didn't know I'd been dating Sheila. We'd kept our relationship quiet because she didn't want her family to find out. Of course, once I met Linda I understood why. I dropped Sheila like a hot potato and asked Linda out. She said yes and then all hell broke loose when Sheila found out. They argued in front of me, Sheila accusing Linda of stealing her boyfriend which wasn't true, of course. In the end, I lost both of them. Linda refused to go out with me again, but by that time Sheila decided to disappear never to be heard from again.'

'She did send a card,' Josh said, 'From Pendry Cove, ever heard of it?'

Martin shook his head. 'Sorry. Where's that?'

'In Devon. Wanted her parents to know she was safe. They went down to find her but she'd left before they got there.'

'Sounds like Sheila. She never did get on with her parents.'

'So you have no idea why she went to Pendry Cove? She never mentioned the place?'

'Sorry, no. As I've already said all she ever went on about was going to London. She had some very fancy ideas did Sheila.' He shook his head. 'Never was satisfied with living in a small market town.'

He stared into space. He was all talked out.

Josh indicated to Megan that it was time to go and they both stood up.

'Thanks for all your help.' He reached in his pocket and handed over a card. 'If you think of anything that might help, just give me a call.'

Martin Coles pushed his large body out of his chair. 'Will do, but I can't think of anything else and after all it was a long time ago. Time doesn't help the brain to remember things.'

'No, I'm sure it doesn't,' Josh said making his way to the front door.

'You never said why you were looking for her,' Martin said as he stood on the doorstep ready to say goodbye.

'Family reunion,' Josh said. 'Linda died a few years ago and her daughter decided it would be nice to have a bit of a family party.'

'Linda has gone? That's a shame. Nice girl. We shared some good times.'

There didn't seem like anything else to say so they said their goodbyes.

'No luck there,' Megan said. 'Where do we go from here?' It seemed as though they'd reached a dead end with no clues as to where to search further.

Josh didn't look happy. 'Not sure. Hopefully, someone we've already spoken to will remember something that will help.'

★ ★ ★

The rest of the day was spent as usual updating records with the interviews they'd done that day. Josh attended to some work he'd been doing for a solicitor and went out for a couple of hours delivering summons to debtors, and when he returned he sat at his desk and just stared into space for a while.

He seemed so far away that Megan decided not to disturb him.

Five o'clock arrived and Megan was thankful that it was the end of the working day.

'I'm off,' she said to Josh who appeared to be doing very little apart from drumming his fingers on his desk and looking at nothing in particular.

'OK.' He rubbed a hand across the stubble on his chin. 'By the way, I won't be in tomorrow.'

She frowned. 'Why?' She hoped he wasn't going to investigate the case further without her.

'I have to take my mother to the hospital for an appointment.'

Megan looked alarmed and remembered that he'd mention something about his mother being ill and that's why he stayed at home after his father died.

'I hope it's nothing serious.'

He shook his head but didn't look at her. 'I hope not. She having a few tests so it could take all day. If there's any problem I'll let you know.

'Send her my best wishes.'

Megan could understand why he was worried. Her own mother was her backbone. Someone she always relied on. She turned and walked out of the office shutting the door softly behind her but not before she heard Josh say, 'Thanks for asking, Megan.'

★ ★ ★

'How is everything?' asked Megan's mother later that evening when she answered her mobile. 'I've not heard from you for a few days,' her mother commented. She wasn't the sort of mother that was continually checking on her daughter but they did like to keep in contact a couple of times a week

'Sorry, Mum. I meant to ring you but I've been so busy sorting stuff out in the office and Josh is letting me help him with a case.' She settled herself down on the sofa ready for a long chat.

'Ooh, sounds exciting. Tell me all about it.'

'Sorry, client confidentiality although I can tell you that it involves finding a missing person.'

'Well, I hope you find whoever it is. So how are things working out with Josh?

147

Last time we spoke you said he was coming round a little bit.'

Megan sighed and took a sip of the coffee she'd just made. 'Not bad. I think there's a slight improvement.'

'Thank goodness for that. I've been imagining you arriving home if things didn't work out.'

'Not going to happen, Mum. You know how stubborn I can be.'

'I certainly do but sometimes it can catch you out, so go careful.'

Megan sighed. Her mother was right about her stubbornness.

'I think Josh has more on his mind than me working with him.' She went on to explain about his mother and how worried he was.

'Poor man. So much going on in his life at the moment. Perhaps you should go easy on him for a while?'

Megan considered it for a moment but he did seem to be coming around to the fact that she wasn't going away any-time soon.

'Oh, Mum, you'll never guess who

I bumped into the other day,' she said changing the subject.

'It wasn't the ghost of Great Uncle Ronald telling you there was another will and you'd not inherited anything?'

Megan rolled her eyes at her mother's attempt at humour. 'No. it was Marcus.'

'What, your ex, Marcus?'

'You sound as surprised as I was when I saw him. When I asked him what he was doing in Keatbury he said he was visiting a friend. I didn't know he knew anyone around here. He certainly didn't when we were going out together.'

'Could be a new friend,' her mother suggested. 'Was he OK with you?'

'Yes, he seemed fine. To be honest we hardly spoke which suited me. It just seemed odd that I bumped into him in the same street where I now live and work.' She sighed, she didn't want to talk about Marcus and told her mother so. 'Tell me all the latest gossip from the neighbourhood.'

Mother and daughter turned their attention to general chatter and another half an hour went by before they said their goodbyes.

Lying in bed that night Megan turned over in her mind the events of the day. She wondered if there were any clues they'd not picked up on during the interviews. There was something niggling in the back of her mind. Something she'd noticed as odd, that she wanted to grab hold of but it slipped away before she could. It just wouldn't come. They needed a decent lead. Time was running out for poor Lily.

She closed her eyes and Josh's face appeared in front of her. He hadn't said what was wrong with his mother but she hoped she was OK. He didn't mention his mother much but from what he said they were close. She decided she would send her a bouquet to wish her well. They'd never met but if she was going to stay in the business it would be a good idea to get to know his family.

11

Megan spent the day working through electoral registers and marriage certificates to no avail. She was hoping she could give Josh some good news but that wasn't the case. 'How did it go?' she asked when he walked in.

'Good, thanks. Better than I hoped.' He seemed to be in a better mood. The worry lines that covered his forehead over the last few weeks appeared to have eased. He even gave her a welcoming smile.

'Really. What is wrong with your mum? I meant to ask but didn't want to sound nosy.'

He looked at her for a moment. 'You could have asked. It's just something I don't talk about.' He scrubbed a hand across his chin and gave out a big sigh. 'To be honest, perhaps I should.'

'I'm a good listener. Go ahead,' Megan said.

'I think I told you that Mum took Dad's death badly? After a few months, I began to notice something different about her. She was still mourning him but she started to get forgetful. Couldn't remember where she put things. Missed appointments. Mumbled to herself. Got cross if she couldn't find something in a cupboard. I began to suspect there was something wrong. You can imagine what I conclusion I came too.'

Megan did, and hoped it wasn't as bad as it sounded.

'Anyway after a lot of persuading she agreed to see a doctor. He decided she should have some tests.' He paused and took in a deep sigh. 'Thankfully she's OK. The doctor thinks it's down to her losing Dad, a bout of depression was the diagnosis. They were so close. Did everything together. The loss was huge for her. Anyway, she began to cut herself off from everybody. I should have noticed but I was working so hard that I didn't have time to notice.' He clenched his fists in frustration, a look of guilt crossing his features.

'There was a lot going on in your life,' Megan pointed out, trying to make him feel better.

'I should have made time for my mother.'

'You did what you could. It's no good blaming yourself. Anyway, you got good news.'

'Yes, and the doctor had a long talk with Mum and told her that she needs to get out more: go for a walk, get some fresh air, make friends or perhaps join a club. Anything to stop brooding.'

'How did she take it?'

'Protested at first.' He chuckled. 'My mother can be quite stubborn when she wants to be. Gradually though she began to listen to the doctor and agreed that she would give it a try.

And because of that she sent you a message'

Megan looked surprised. 'Me? I don't even know your mum. Why would she send me a message?'

'That's exactly why. She thinks it's

153

been remiss of her not inviting you to dinner to get to know you.'

Megan smiled. 'Oh, that's nice of her.'

'So how about it? Dinner tonight?' He looked slightly guilty. 'I know it's a bit short notice but when she suggested it I thought why not strike whilst the iron's hot. You haven't got any other plans, have you?'

She should have been mad at him for accepting an invitation on her behalf but he looked so hopeful that she decided against it. She picked up her desk diary and ran her fingers along with today's page before looking up at him. 'You're in luck. My diary is empty for this evening.' She snapped the diary shut and wagged a finger at him. 'Just don't do it again. I might have made other arrangements.' She smiled to take the sting out of her words.

What other arrangements she could have she didn't know. The only friend she'd made since moving here was Sarah. Still, Josh didn't know that. He hardly knew anything about her personal life.

For that matter, she knew little about his.

'Thanks, Megan I appreciate it. I'll pick you up at seven, if that's OK,' he said, sounding relieved.

'No, I'll drive myself. Save you coming out.'

'You're sure?'

'Positive. I can't wait to meet her. Now, let's go over what I did yesterday.'

The conversation turned to more mundane things. A couple of jobs were received the day before which pleased Josh no end but he was a little disappointed that the Sheila White case seemed to have stalled.

'We'll leave it for today and hopefully tomorrow we'll find a lead we can work on.'

★ ★ ★

Josh seem more relaxed since he'd told her about his mother, Megan mused as she got ready that evening. She ran a coat of lipstick across her lips and checked herself in the mirror. Not wanting to look overdressed she'd decided on a black skirt along with a favourite scarlet sweater. Happy with her appearance she shrugged on her coat and picked up her car keys.

It wasn't difficult to find Josh's house. A small private estate on the outskirts of town with large detached houses. Nothing like the small terraced house Megan shared with her mother.

Josh took after his mother. There was a welcome smile on her face and a dimple just like his. Her hair hadn't hit the grey streaks yet and dark locks cupped her face in a pixie style which suited her.

'Welcome. I'm so sorry I haven't invited you before, but Josh said you were busy settling in.'

Megan cast a glance over at Josh who stood to one side of his mother. He shrugged but said nothing which Megan took to mean that he hadn't wanted to upset his mother until a diagnosis had been made. She could understand that and it pleased her that he put his mother's needs before others.

Megan went to shake Marie Rayne's hand, but instead, she was wrapped in the woman's arms in a welcoming hug.

Josh took her coat and Marie ushered her into the sitting room. 'Sit down, my dear.' She turned to her son. 'Josh, get Megan a drink. Dinner will be about half an hour but I thought we could sit and have a chat before then.'

'Lovely,' Megan agreed and looked over a Josh. 'Just an orange juice, please. I'm driving.'

'I'll have the same,' Marie said, settling down in a chair opposite Megan. 'So, I'm sure you were surprised when Ronnie decided to leave you his half of the business?'

Megan gave Josh a swift look as he placed her drink in her hand. Had he mentioned how upset he was to his mother? He must have understood her unspoken question and shook his head slightly, indicating that that wasn't the case.

'It certainly was. I only knew Great

Uncle Ronald vaguely from my child-hood and not set eyes on him in years. I must have made quite an impression on him.'

'Strange man, Ronnie, if you don't mind me saying so.'

'Not at all. As I said, I don't remember much about him but I understand he was quite a character?'

'Oh, he was that alright.' Marie chuckled. 'Some of the things he did drove my late husband up the wall, but he worked hard in those days.'

'Pity he didn't carry on working hard after Dad died,' Josh muttered, luckily not loud enough for his mother to hear.

'I hope I work hard,' Megan said. 'I don't want to let our side of the family down. She smiled. 'Although I must admit Josh has done a lot to upgrade the office equipment which makes it much easier on the clerical side.'

'He's a good son.' She looked at Josh lovingly.

Megan grinned at his cheeks going red.

'It needed to be done, Mum,' he said, a bit too gruffly.

'I know son. I'm proud of you. I'm sure you'll keep your father's legacy going.'

'I'll do my best.' He reached over and squeezed his mother's hand.

Marie turned back to Megan. 'What did you do before you became an apprentice detective?'

'I worked in a flower shop, arranging bouquets for weddings and special occasions.'

'Oh, how lovely.' Marie beamed. 'Do you know I've always considered it a special art to be able to do those arrangements?'

Megan smiled. 'It's not that hard. I hadn't a clue before I started the job.' She laughed. 'Didn't even know what some of the flowers were called. You should take it up. It can be very therapeutic.' She glanced across at Josh wondering if she should have mentioned therapy, but he seemed to be OK with her words.

She shouldn't have worried. He looked across at her with a smile of approval.

'Sounds interesting. What do you think, Mum? Fancy having a go?'

A frown appeared on the older woman's face. 'I don't know. It sounds a bit complicated and I'm far too old to learn many new things.'

'Nonsense,' Megan interjected. 'I bet there's a course in town for beginners. Why don't you take a class and see if you like it?'

'Great idea,' Josh said immediately pulling out his mobile phone from his pocket and tapping away. 'There's a class at the local library in the evenings, Mum. A six-week course starting this coming Thursday.'

Marie bit down on her lip and Megan could see she was trying to find an excuse not to go, but hadn't Josh said the doctor wanted her to get out and about and stop moping at home? She could see the hope in Josh's eyes slowly fade as his mother looked undecided.

'How about I go with you?' Megan suggested. 'See if you like it. Nothing ventured and all that. To be honest I've missed putting together a beautiful bouquet or an arrangement of fresh flowers. My mother used to love the ones I did for our house. You'd be doing me a favour if you came with me.'

Marie pondered for a moment and Megan could see she was considering whether to say yes or no. She must have come to a decision because she said, 'I suppose it would be good to see fresh flowers in the house again. Josh's dad used to buy me a bunch every week.' Her eyes twinkled. 'Mainly from the garage on the way home from the office but it's the thought that counts, isn't it?'

'It certainly is. So how about it? Shall we go?'

A smile spread across Marie's face and she raised her hands in defeat. 'OK, you've persuaded me. Josh, would you be a love and book two places?' She stood up. 'Now, I'd better dish up supper before it gets ruined.' She left the room refusing any help from Megan.

'Thanks for that,' Josh said, putting away his phone after booking two places.

'It's just what she needs. Are you sure you're not putting yourself out?'

Megan shook her head. 'I wouldn't have offered if I didn't have the time, and I meant what I said, I do miss it.'

'All the same, thanks for helping out. I'm sure it will do her the world of good.'

'No problem.'

The meal was delicious and Marie was a good hostess, recalling tales of many cases that Ronnie and her husband worked on.

The evening was drawing to a close when Josh's mobile rang. Megan was in the kitchen with his mother. Josh could hear them laughing about something or other. He admitted to himself that Megan was doing a good job of cheering his mother up. He looked at his phone not recognising the number. It was late and he wasn't sure who would be ringing him at this time of the evening.

'Hello. Josh Rayne.'

'Hi, it's Jerry Deakes, we met a few days ago.'

'Hi, Jerry. I remember. Good to hear

from you.'

'You asked me to contact you if I came up with anything to do with Natalie. It just came to me as I was watching the TV. It might not be anything, but when Natalie was here we went to the fair. She loved it. Didn't stop talking about it for days afterwards. She said she wouldn't mind getting a job with them. She left the same night that the fair did. She could have gone with them so it might be worth following up.'

A lead at last! Josh tried to keep the excitement out of his voice. 'Thanks, Jerry, sounds promising. I don't suppose you remember the name of the funfair do you?'

'Yes, it just so happens I do because it always reminds me of my name. Dickens Fun Fair. They used to come and set up just outside Pendry Cove every year up until about five years ago. Although I must confess I never did visit the fair after Natalie left. To be honest I'm not keen on them myself.' He chuckled. 'Not my scene. Anyway, as I said I hope it helps in you trying to find her.'

'Fingers crossed. Thanks.'

Megan was just coming out of the kitchen as Josh disconnected the call. At her enquiring look, he raised his phone. 'That was Jerry Deakes. He remembered something. Tomorrow we go searching for funfairs.'

'Funfairs?' Megan said, looking puzzled.

Josh puffed out his chest, his eyes bright with excitement. 'Sheila might have joined the funfair after she left Pendry Cove.'

Megan's eyes widened. 'A definite clue?'

'It sounds hopeful. Yes, I think we have a clue.'

Megan wasn't surprised. From all she'd learnt about Sheila White, the idea of being involved in any sort of entertainment was just up the young girl's street.

'Better get home and have a good night's sleep then.'

'Oh, are you going so soon, dear?' Marie said as she came out of the kitchen and overheard Megan's words.

Megan nodded. 'Thanks for a lovely evening. I'll see you Thursday for the start of those classes. Do you know, I'm quite excited to be going.'

'Funnily enough, so am I,' Marie said, smiling. 'Something to look forward to.'

She said her goodbyes and Josh saw her to her car. 'Thanks for tonight,' he said as she unlocked the door to her car.

She smiled at him. 'It's no trouble. Your mum is a lovely lady, and fingers crossed the flower arranging classes will help her.'

He looked at her for a long moment before surprising her by pulling her into his arms and gently brushing his lips against hers. She shivered at the sensation.

'See you in the morning,' he whispered before letting her go and opening the car door for her.

Without another word he walked back inside shutting the front door behind him, not once looking back. She touched her fingers to her lips. The kiss was brief but the feel of his lips on hers lingered.

The sensation was still there as she readied herself for bed later. She didn't want to be attracted to him, but felt that it was a little too late for that.

12

Every day since she'd asked them to help find her aunt, Allison Frampton was on the phone wanting an update. 'Any news?'

'Not yet.' Megan didn't want to sound despondent but she heard a sigh on the other end of the line so hurriedly said. 'But we have a few leads that we're are working on'

'I just don't understand how she could disappear like that. I know I shouldn't pin all my hopes on her being a match, but I've just got a feeling she's the answer to our prayers.'

Megan wasn't much into feelings. Hard facts were much better in her opinion but she couldn't say that to the woman who was worried about her daughter's health. Yesterday she'd told Megan that Lily was getting worse. For once, Megan was at loss as to what to say.

'We have a lead we're going to check

up on today,' she told Allison now.

It wouldn't hurt to give the woman something positive to hold on to. She looked across at Josh who was checking on the internet to try and find the funfair that Jerry mentioned the night before. She wondered if he would mention the kiss this morning but it was business as usual when he walked in the office. She decided that it was a spur of the moment action on his part and was surprised how disappointed she felt about that.

'I hope its good news. Let me know as soon as you know something,' Allison said bringing Megan out of her musings.

'Will do,' Megan said before saying goodbye.

'I've found them,' Josh announced, a few minutes later pointing to his computer screen. 'Dickens Amusements are at Little Westbridge for the next fortnight.'

'Never heard of the place. Where is it?'

'About an hour and half from here.' He frowned, looking at the screen. 'Doesn't look as though there's a phone number so we can't call them.' He stood up and reached for his jacket. 'Come on, get your coat.'

Megan looked astonished. 'What, now? You want us to go straight away?'

'No time like the present and if that was Allison Frampton I heard you talking too on the phone you did promise her some good news.'

'Let's hope we can deliver,' she said, shrugging on her coat and grabbing her handbag as she followed Josh out of the office.

* * *

Thinking it was a small village Megan was surprised to see Little Westbridge was, in fact, a small town. The funfair was easy enough to find, set out on a hill overlooking the town. Bright lights flashed across the horizon and loud music blasted through the air. She could hear screeches and screams from people being flung up in the air in monstrous machines or chomping their way through sticks of pink candyfloss. Everyone was having fun.

Quickly establishing who the owner was and a request to talk to him, they were told to wait.

'Do you think he'll be able to help us?' Megan asked.

Before Josh could answer a man in his thirties dressed in jeans and a black t-shirt approached them. 'Danny Dickens, you wanted to see me?'

He seemed wary and Josh quickly explained why they wanted to speak to him. It seemed to put him at his ease and he looked at the photograph of Sheila. Danny scratched his head before giving it a shake.

'Sorry, a bit before my time. I've been involved in the fair all my life, but can't say I remember this girl.'

'She went by the name of Natalie although her real name was Sheila.' Josh hoped that saying the two names might jog the man's memory.

Danny looked at the photograph again before handing it back. 'Sorry, nothing comes to mind.'

They both looked disappointed until he said. 'But my dad might be able to help you. He's retired now, but keeps scrap books of all the people who worked for us over the years. Follow me.' He led them to a large caravan at the back of the fair and told them to wait while he spoke to his father.

'Do you think he'll be able to help?' Megan asked when Danny disappeared inside the caravan.

Josh looked hopeful. 'Keep your fingers crossed. It's the best lead we've had so far.'

That was true. Every tiny lead was improving their chances of finding the missing woman.

Danny emerged from the trailer and stood on the steps beckoning them inside. Danny's dad, Eddie, sat on an old rocking chair, a cap pulled back on his head, his sleeves rolled up, nursing a large mug of tea in his hand. Danny lent forwarded and shouted in his ear. 'These are the people I was telling you about, Dad.'

The old man looked up, studying them.

'He's bit deaf,' Danny said, 'But you're OK if you talk right at him in a loud voice.

'I can hear perfectly well,' the old man said, giving his son a look that said he wasn't too old to be reprimanded. He looked at Josh. 'You have a picture of this woman you're looking for? What's she done? Not in trouble I hope. I don't grass on old employees, not unless its murder.' He chuckled and then his face went serious. 'She hasn't has she? Killed someone?'

'No, nothing like that,' Josh quickly assured him. 'Her family are looking for her. Just want to know if she's OK.'

'Hmm.'The old man scrutinised them for a moment before making a decision. 'You have a picture?' he asked again.

Josh pulled the photograph from his jacket pocket and handed it over to the old man. 'Do you recognise her?' he asked after Eddie studied the image for

172

a few moments.

'What did you say her name was?'

'Sheila White, although she may have changed her name to Natalie.'

Eddie looked back at the photograph. He put down his mug of tea and tapped the picture with his forefinger. 'Natalie was the name she went by when she worked for me, or rather she became Madame Mystery. Danny, pass me the silver scrap book on the shelf.' Eddie leafed through the book until he stopped at a page. He tapped a photograph before holding it out to Josh. 'Madam Mystery, best fortune teller I ever hired.'

Josh looked at the picture. He could just make out that it was Sheila, although she was dressed in a long black skirt, a purple shawl wrapped around her shoulders, gold bangles hung from her wrists and she wore large hooped earrings.

'In those days in every fair there was a fortune teller,' Eddie said as Josh passed the book over to Megan. 'Brought in a lot of trade. Young girls wanting to find out if they were going to marry a millionaire or find the love of their life. Madam Mystery was good at telling them what they wanted to hear. Of course, we don't have those sort of acts these days. More's the pity.' He glanced at his son and shook his head.

'Kids today don't want that sort of thing, Dad.' Danny said, shaking his head. 'We've been over this before. We have to look to the future.'

'The future,' Eddie scoffed. 'Bring back the old days is what I say.'

'So, what happened to Madam Mystery, or rather Natalie?' Josh asked, not wanting to get into a family argument about what was best, the past or the present.

'She was with us for about five years then met someone and moved on. Brian Mathers as I recall.' He tapped his forehead. 'Might be old but I've got a good memory for names. Always have. He worked for us one summer. We used take on local workers in the towns we visited. Anyway they were romancing so she decided to stay. Must have found her own millionaire.' He chuckled at his attempt at a joke.

'Do you remember where?'

Eddie screwed his eyes up trying to remember. 'Packforth, as I recall. Little town in the Midlands.'

He yawned and lent back in his chair closing his eyes.

'I think Dad's a bit tired now,' said Danny, putting a hand on his dad's shoulder.

'Yes, of course', said Megan. 'We'll be getting on. Thanks for your help.'

'A real clue at last,' Megan said, her voice full of excitement as they headed back to the car. 'Do you know where Packforth is? Never heard of it myself.'

Josh unlocked the car. 'It's not far from us, about forty-five minutes. Come on let's get home and check the electoral register. I think you're right we have a real clue at long last. We're getting close, Megan. I can feel it in my bones.'

Megan laughed. Josh looked excited and she was swept away by his enthusiasm. They headed back down the motorway discussing what they needed to do when they arrived back at the office.

★ ★ ★

Megan quickly turned on her computer and began a search of the electoral register, the quickest way they both felt in finding someone.

'We're in luck,' she cried after only a few minutes. 'There's a Brian Mathers living in Packforth.' She frowned. 'Although he's not married. Single it says here.' She was disappointed. She felt sure that Sheila would have married and settled down.

Josh came over and looked over her shoulder. She felt her stomach do another flip. Why was it doing that? She shouldn't be affected by his closeness. She pulled herself together and pointed to the information on the screen.

'Could be living together. It's not that unusual in this day and age. Check for a Sheila White or a Natalie White.'

Megan ran her fingers across the

176

screen but there was nothing. She sat back in her chair feeling dejected.

Josh rested a hand on her shoulder giving it a gentle squeeze. 'We're not giving up. Look, I'll ring this guy and see if he remembers Sheila. It may be he knows where she is. She may have even changed her name again. Pretty elusive is our Sheila White.'

Unfortunately Josh couldn't find a phone number for Brian Mathers. 'Must be ex-directory,' he said. 'Looks like we have another trip on our hands. We'll go tomorrow, it's not far from here.'

Megan had really hoped she would be able to give Allison Frampton some good news after today's visit.

Josh surprised her with his next words. 'It's getting late. How about we go out for something to eat? I doubt you want to cook tonight after being out all day.'

He was right, she didn't feel like cooking. 'OK, why not?'

'Great. I'll ring Mum. She's out tonight so I'd have to cook for myself.'

Megan looked surprised. 'I thought

your mother never went out.'

'She announced this morning that she'd phoned one of her old friends and was invited out for the evening.'

'Good for her!'

'It surprised me as well, but I think it's all down to you. She's really looking forward to going to that class with you tomorrow. I think she realised what she's missing. Meeting up with an old friend is a small step but at least it's something.'

'I'm glad.'

'Me too.' The dimple appeared at the side of Josh's cheek as he smiled. 'Come on, turn off your computer and get your coat. There's a nice little Italian restaurant just outside of town. It's early so we should be able to get a table easily. How do you like pasta?'

'Love it,' Megan said, grabbing her coat and following him outside.

Josh must have used the restaurant frequently from the friendly greeting he received as they entered the restaurant.

'Luigi, meet Megan,' Josh said to the small grey haired man who clasped his hand in a firm grip. Luigi's dark eyes sparkled as he reached out and surprised Megan by kissing her on both cheeks. Josh turned to Megan. 'Luigi's son and I were at school together. How is William?'

'He's doing well. His new restaurant seems to be a hit.'

'William followed his father into the restaurant business,' Josh explained when Megan looked puzzled. 'They're both excellent chefs.'

'His compliments are always welcome and because of that I shall offer you the best seat in the house.'

Both men laughed with Megan joining in. Luigi did indeed find them a good table by the window.

'Would you like to try my new pasta dish?' Luigi smacked his lips together. 'The sauce is divine, if I say so myself.'

'Sounds good,' Megan said, laughing at Luigi's dramatics.

'I'll have the same,' Josh said, chuckling along. 'Now, go and cook and leave us in peace.'

Luigi bowed. 'Certainly, Sir.' he said,

giving Megan a wink before walking off. Megan eyes followed him until he disappeared behind a door before turning her attention back to Josh.

'He's a good friend,' Josh explained. A waiter appeared with a bottled of wine. 'Compliments of the house,' he said to Josh before popping the cork and handing it to him.

'Just right,' Josh said breathing in the fragrant aroma as he held the cork to his nose.

The waiter poured two glasses and left the bottle on the table.

'Cheers.' Josh raised his glass and Megan followed suit. 'To a successful day tomorrow.'

'I'll drink to that,' Megan said, raising the glass to her lips and tasting the refreshing liquid. 'Ooh, lovely and crisp, just the way I like it.'

A couple of people passed their table. Megan looked up and was surprised to see Marcus walking towards a small alcove following another man she didn't recognise. He didn't appear to have seen her, for which she was thankful. She carried on staring, thinking how strange it was that after not seeing him since they split up she'd now seen him twice and in a town some distance from his own.

'Something wrong?' Josh asked, looking over his shoulder to see what she was staring at. A man about his own age with fair hair sat in an alcove talking to someone by his side whom Josh couldn't see.

She turned her attention back to Josh. 'Nothing really, just my ex, Marcus Rowland deciding to eat at the same restaurant as us. I'm just surprised to see him that's all.'

'Bad breakup?'

Megan took another sip of her wine and avoided looking at Josh. 'Let's just say it didn't end well.'

'So you're off men at the moment?' he said, trying to lighten the mood that suddenly became a little intense.

She fiddled with her wine glass but didn't say anything more.

'We can eat somewhere else if it's a problem,' he offered. He didn't want her to feel uncomfortable when all he'd wanted to do was for them both to relax over a well cooked meal.

She looked up and shrugged. 'No, it's fine. We've both moved on. Anyway it doesn't appear that he's seen me. Let's enjoy our meal.' She frowned. 'Strange though, it's the second time I've seen him since I moved here.' She took a sip of her wine. 'I meant to ask you about Mr Blackstone who rang the other day.' She tilted her head towards the alcove. 'Marcus works for his firm. Funny that, don't you think?'

Josh looked over at Marcus again. 'Not really. Blackstone's is a big organisation with many employees.'

'I suppose so,' she agreed. 'Anyway what's the case about? You haven't told me yet.'

Josh raised his hands. 'That's enough of talking about work for today. Can we talk out something else?'

He didn't want to discuss any cases tonight and happily Megan agreed. Their food arrived and they both turned their attention to the delicious plate of pasta placed in front of them. For the remainder of the meal their conversation turned to their likes and dislikes. Megan was surprised that they both like 60's music and there was a happy debate about who was the best group, The Beatles or the Rolling Stones.

'OK, we'll agree to differ,' Megan said grinning as she finished off her meal and drained the last of her wine. She felt heady and realised that she'd drank most of it, Josh sticking to just one glass because he was driving. She yawned and looked at her watch, surprised to see that time was moving swiftly on.

'My bedtime, I think,' she said.

'I'll get you home in no time. We have another long day ahead of us tomorrow.'

Josh helped her on with her coat and she cast another glance at Marcus. He was deep in conversation with the other man and all through the meal didn't look in her direction, for which she was grateful, but once again she thought it was odd that she seemed to be bumping

into him so often when it hadn't happened at all when she lived at home.

★ ★ ★

Inside Luigi's, Marcus watched as the
door to the restaurant closed behind
Josh and Megan. He turned his attention
back to Terry Cuthbert, his companion.
'Well, what do you think, are they onto
us?'

Terry sat back in his chair and
drummed his fingers against the table-
cloth. 'Not sure but we'll keep an eye
on them. So far Josh Rayne hasn't been
snooping about. If so I'm sure my uncle
would have mentioned it.' Terry stared
hard at Marcus. 'Next time you have
a girlfriend make sure she doesn't see
anything she shouldn't, it could cost
Cuthbert's a lot of money.'

Marcus looked uncomfortable. He'd
been stupid leaving his laptop open. He
was usually so careful.

It was also his bad luck that Megan
was now working with Josh Rayne. He

184

couldn't believe it when he bumped into her outside Merriweather and Rayne a few weeks ago and she told him what she was doing. He needed to be careful and as Terry said, keep an eye on both Josh and Megan, there was too much to lose.

'Don't worry,' he said now, 'She hasn't remembered anything yet. She may not have even seen anything, but if anything does come of it and she remembers I can deal with her.'

'Maybe so,' Terry said, scooping up another forkful of pasta, 'But what about Josh Rayne, he's no pushover.' He popped the pasta in his mouth and began to chew.

'It will be sorted,' Marcus assured the other man. 'I can handle one nosy private detective.' Terry Cuthbert raised an eyebrow. 'I hope you're right.' Marcus cross two fingers under the table. He hoped so too.

13

Hearing footsteps Josh looked up to see Megan walking down the street carrying two travel cups of coffee.

'I know you want to get off early so I decided I'd treat us to a coffee from Sarah's café.' She passed one to him.

'Thanks,' he said taking a sip.

She seemed in a happier mood this morning. He'd notice that after seeing her ex-boyfriend the previous night she'd lapsed into silence during the ride home. Was she still carrying a torch for him? She hadn't said so and he didn't like to ask — after all it was none of his business. Or was it? He recalled the kiss they'd shared outside his house. It was an impulsive move on his part, although he didn't regret it and decided not to bring the subject up the next morning in case Megan brushed it off as a thank you kiss, which he realised later it certainly wasn't.

'I have a really good feeling about today,' she said, as she hooked her seatbelt over her shoulder before locking it into place. 'I do hope we can give Allison some good news.'

'So do I. Fingers crossed we can find Sheila today and be home by lunchtime.'

'That'll be good. Don't forget I'm going flower arranging with your mum tonight. How is she? Not nervous?'

'I think she might be. She was trying to get out of going this morning. Indicated that she had a migraine coming on and might not make it.'

Megan looked shocked. 'Oh no. Is she OK?'

Josh smiled and shook his head. 'She's fine. I think meeting up with her friend yesterday was a bit much for her, hence the pretend migraine. In reality she just wants to put off going, but I saw through the pretence and told her she was going and that was that, even if I have to carry her there.'

'Oh, dear,' she laughed, 'A bit of a drastic measure don't you think?'

'Not at all. I know my mother very well and if she thinks she can get out of something she will.' He tapped the side of his nose. 'Not this time.'

'Let's hope you're right.'

They settled into a comfortable silence. The town wasn't far and within the hour they arrived at a small cul de sac at the edge of town.

Josh crossed his fingers and held them in the air. 'For good luck,' he said, turning off the engine and stepping out of the car.

Megan followed him down a small pathway to the front door and stood beside him as he rang the bell.

'Doesn't look as though anyone's at home,' he said when nobody opened the door.

'Try again.'

Josh did so but there was still no response.

'Are you looking for the owner?' a voice called from above. They both looked up at a woman who was poking her head through a window of the house next door.

'Yes, Brian Mathers. I believe he lives here.'

'Sorry, love not anymore. Moved away about six months ago.'

Oh no, not another disappointment.

'Do you know where?'

'Hang on love. I'll come down. All this shouting is no good for my poor old throat.'

The woman emerged a few moments later, duster and a tin of polish in her hand. 'You caught me doing the housework.' She stepped outside the door. 'Now, what's this about Brian?'

Josh quickly explained that they wanted to talk to him about someone he might know. A woman. He held out the picture of Sheila. 'Do you recognise her?'

'Just a minute, let me get my glasses.' She disappeared inside only to come a few minutes later. 'Right, let's have a look.' She looked closely at the picture, a frown appearing across her brow. 'I could be mistaken because this is an old photograph but I'd say that's his wife.'

'Sorry did you say wife? Josh looked puzzled.

'That's right. Sheila,' The woman handed the photograph back after having another close look at it. 'Yes, that's Sheila. Of course, she's a lot older and a lot thicker around the waist, but then aren't we all?' She laughed at her own joke.

They were married and Natalie was now back to Sheila! How confusing, thought Megan, although it didn't answer the question why the woman wasn't on any electoral register over the past decades. There were so many unanswered questions relating to this case.

'I didn't realise Sheila was married,' Josh said.

'Oh, they haven't been married long, did the deed, sold the house and moved on within the space of about six weeks. It was done all very quickly. Been going out together for years but only decided to get hitched when Brian retired and they wanted to travel.'

'Travel?'

190

'Yes, that's right. Brian always wanted to take a trip along the canals. Always said that he could see the whole of the country from a boat. Anyway, he sold up and bought one of the narrow boats and off they went. It all seemed a bit of a rush to me but Brian said he'd waited long enough for an adventure, so off they went.'

'Any idea where? We must find Sheila. We have some information for her.'

The woman shook her head. 'Sorry, no. Not been left a load of money by an ageing aunt or something, has she?' The woman looked at Josh expectantly.

'Could be.' Josh said nothing more hoping the woman would help him out.

'If it's that important try down at the lock outside town. They might be able to help you. I know Brian's boat was moored there before they headed off. An extended honeymoon Sheila called it.'

Josh decided they'd got all the information they were going to get from the woman and thanked her for her time. He handed her a card just in case she remembered anything else that might help them but he doubted that would happen.

Megan looked a little despondent when they got in the car.

'This is just a stumbling block. They always appear when you're carrying out an investigation,' he said when he saw her shoulders sag.

'I really did think we'd find her today,' Megan said. She'd so hoped that she could give Allison the news she was hoping for. Yet again they would have to tell her that her aunt was just out of their grasp. 'I've just realised that Brian Mathers must have added his details to the electoral register before their marriage.' She frowned. 'Although it doesn't explain why Sheila's name doesn't appear anywhere.'

'Yes, that is strange. On a more positive note, we know a lot more now.'

'Like what?'

'We know she's alive.'

'Did you think otherwise?'

'I did think there was a possibility.

Thank goodness I was wrong.'

He turned on the engine. 'Come on let's see if we can find out anything at the lock.

They found the place easily enough and the man in charge remembered the couple. 'Excited they were. Couldn't wait to get started. Renamed the barge *Second Chance* and off they went.'

'Any idea where?'

The man pulled off his woolly hat and scratched his head. 'Said something about heading for the Norfolk Broads first but that was a while back. To be honest they could be anywhere by now.'

Josh thanked the man and they returned to the car deciding to stop for something to eat before heading home. Josh found a pub which sold hot food just off the motorway and they settled down with a drink after they ordered their food.

'So, where do we go from here?' Megan said. She was fed up. All this chasing about and still they were no further forward. When would they get a break?

Josh must have sensed her mood and reached out and squeezed her hand. 'Hey. We'll get there. Sometimes these things take time and patience. No one said it would be easy.'

'That's for sure,' she huffed, 'But we need a better plan than just following dead ends. Perhaps they have to register with authorities of where they intend to travel?'

Josh pulled out his phone and got onto the internet to search for information before shaking his head. 'Apart from getting a licence you can go anywhere you want.' He turned off his phone. 'Looks like we'll have to think of another plan.'

'Any ideas?'

'Not at the moment.' He didn't have a clue where to go from here, but decided to keep the thought to himself. He reached for his drink. 'Don't worry, by tomorrow morning I'll have a plan.' He took a sip of his drink hoping he was telling Megan the truth, because at the moment his mind was a blank canvas.

★ ★ ★

It was late when Josh pulled up outside the office. 'I'll go straight home. I'll pick you up later and get you and Mum to the community centre.'

'It's no bother, Josh. I'll come to your house and collect your mother.'

'You're sure?'

'No problem at all. The class starts at seven. Tell your mum to be ready for six-thirty.' She picked up her handbag and stepped out of the car. Josh raised a hand, put the car into gear and drove off, leaving her standing on the pavement watching the car disappear out of sight before pulling out her key fob to unlock the front door.

She was surprised to find that the front door was ajar. She was certain she'd pulled it shut before she went to collect the coffees that morning.

She wondered if she should call Josh back just in case someone had broken into the office. Although she couldn't

imagine why. There was nothing valu-
able in there apart from the computer
system and she supposed that it might
be attractive to any burglar.

She pushed open the door and slowly
walked inside. It didn't look as though
anything was disturbed in the hallway.

The office door was shut but she
opened it cautiously just in case. She
didn't realise that she was holding her
breath until she let out a deep sigh. Nothing looked out of place. She couldn't
have shut the door properly.

Then she another thought: what about
her flat?

She slowly climbed the stairs and gave
another sigh of relief when she saw that
the door was firmly closed. She stepped
inside.

Everything looked the same as it did
when she'd left that morning. As she
walked further into her tiny flat she
sensed there was something different but
couldn't put a finger on it. She pushed
away the feeling, she was just being
silly. As far as she could see there was

196

nothing missing, nothing disturbed. She was imagining things when there wasn't anything to worry about.

She made herself a hot drink and settled herself down on the sofa, and began making notes of the information they'd collected during the day. She'd update the records on her computer in the morning.

★ ★ ★

Marie Rayne looked apprehensive when Megan picked her up that evening. She held onto her handbag like a lifeline, twisting the strap first one way then the other.

Megan laid a hand on her arm. 'Come on, you'll enjoy it,' she said, giving the other woman's hand an encouraging squeeze.

'I know I'm just being silly. I never used to be this nervous.'

'It's OK being nervous. It's the same with me. I always get nervous when I meet new people.' She looked over at

Josh who stood in the hallway behind his mother. 'I was terrified when I first met your son!' she teased.

'Josh?' Marie sounded surprised then saw the smile on Megan's face and chuckled herself.

'Go on the pair of you before I turn into a big bad wolf,' Josh growled at both of them sending them into fits of laughter and breaking the tension.

The class was small with only eight women of different ages attending. They'd been told to bring their own flowers and a block of flower foam. Marie supplied the flowers and some greenery, as instructed by Megan, who'd supplied the flower foam.

Their tutor was a middle-aged woman and good at giving instructions. She made all the women feel at ease. Megan watched as Marie began to relax and enjoy herself even chatting to the woman who sat next to her. They were about the same age and seemed to have some things in common.

At the end of the night, they both

created two elegant displays and Marie made a new friend.

As she settled herself next to Megan in the car she gave a beaming smile. 'Thanks for taking me, Megan I enjoyed myself. It's surprising how much I've missed going out and being in the company of other people. Did Josh tell you I went to visit an old friend yesterday? It was a small step and not nearly as frightening as tonight.'

'You've done well on both occasions,' Megan said kindly. 'You've been through a lot in the last couple of years, and it takes time to move one.'

'You're right, it does, but I think it's time. I know Josh has been worried about me. He doesn't say much but it's been a strain on him these last few years. Working hard at the business and then finding out about Ronnie's will and you. So much on his shoulders.' She looked a little sad. 'Hopefully I won't be a burden to him anymore.'

'I'm sure he never thinks of you as a burden,' Megan was quick to assure the other woman.

'All the same, I haven't helped matters. So, as from today, things are going to change. I'm going out for coffee tomorrow morning with Jenny, the woman I was talking to.'

'Excellent,' Megan said. 'Come on, let's get you home and tell Josh your news. Plus, he's going to like your effort at flower arranging.' They both looked over at the two flower arrangements which lay on the back seat.

'Yours looks so much better than mine,' Marie said, shaking her head.

'Hey, yours looks great and I do have a few years of practice to draw on. Don't worry, a few more lessons and you'll be a professional.'

They both laughed and were still laughing when they pulled up outside Marie's home.

Josh must have been worried as he was out of the front door before Megan turned off the engine.

'How did it go?' He looked anxious but the look quickly disappeared from his face when he saw his mother's bright face full of laughter.

'Very well. Can't wait to go again next week.'

Josh looked over the roof of the car and mouthed thank you to Megan. She smiled. 'See you tomorrow,' she said as she handed Marie her flower arrangement and got back in her car.

'Not staying for coffee?' Josh asked.

'Not tonight. I'm tired. See you in the morning.'

He watched until her car disappeared. He really wanted to kiss her again, but not out of gratitude. He wanted the kiss for himself. When this case was over they'd have a long talk about feelings.

14

Josh announced as he walked into the office the following morning, 'We need to talk to Allison and her husband.'

Megan agreed. 'Good idea. We need to give them an update on where we are with the search or not as is the case.'

'No, not that. I have something else in mind.'

She gave him a questioning look but said nothing, just reached for the phone. 'I'll give Allison a call. See if it's convenient.'

Josh waved her suggestion away. 'No need, I rang on the way here. She says we can go this morning. Lily's out of hospital and Graham, her husband, is at home so it works out well.'

They hadn't met Lily before. She'd been in hospital when Allison came to see them and although Megan suggested they meet her Allison blocked the idea, stating that while Lily was having treatment visitors weren't encourage due to the possibility of infection.

'How is she?' Megan asked.

'Not too bad, according to Allison. Whatever treatment they gave her in hospital seemed to have helped, although according to her mother it's only a short term solution and it's still urgent that she gets a donor.'

'Still no luck with the donor bank?'

Josh shook his head.

'So what's the plan?'

He opened the office door. 'I'll tell you on the way there. We have to stop at a stationers. Lily likes colouring books according to her mum so I thought we'd go bearing gifts. A few coloured pencils wouldn't go amiss either.'

'Good idea,' Megan said. She pulled on her coat, grabbed her bag and chased after Josh who was already out of the door. The man was always in a rush!

In the end they bought half a dozen colouring books which Megan just knew Lily would just love and the biggest box of colouring pencils Josh could find.

'The girl needs spoiling,' he said when Megan gave him a look that told him he was indulging the child but she agreed. Lily deserved spoiling.

Graham Frampton opened the door to them.

He didn't look like a man in his thirties. The constant worry over his daughter's health was aging him. His dark hair was going grey and there were deep worry lines across his forehead.

Allison didn't look much better. Dark shadows hung underneath her eyes.

Megan wanted to reach out and hug them both and assure them that everything would be OK — only she couldn't promise that at all. In fact at the moment she couldn't promise anything.

Instead she put a smile on her face and walked inside the house hoping that the parents would go for the idea Josh outlined to her on the way over to the house. She wasn't sure if they would go for it but Josh assured her that he could be very persuasive when he wanted to be.

Lily lay on the sofa in the living room, a blanket over her legs. She looked thin for her age and her skin was pale but she smiled in delight when Josh handed over the gift they'd brought for her.

'Thank you,' she said in a quiet voice after she'd looked at her parents to see if it was OK for her accept. She quickly set about sorting out the crayons and thumbing through the pages of the different colouring books before deciding to settle on a book of animals.

'Not surprised she picked that one,' Graham said. 'She loves her animals. Wants to be a vet went she's grown up. Isn't that right, Lily?'

The little girl gave a toothy smile and went back to her colouring ignoring the grown-ups.

'That's if she makes it that far,' Megan heard Allison say in a very quiet voice.

Graham put an arm around his wife's shoulders. 'It'll be fine,' he assured her.

His wife gave him a weak smile before turning her attention to Josh. 'Now you said on the phone you wanted to talk to us both,' She gestured for them to move away out of ear shot of Lily. 'You said you hadn't any luck in finding Aunt Sheila so what do you suggest we do now?'

'I told Allison it was a waste of time,' Graham said trying to keep the irritation out of his voice. 'The woman just doesn't want to be found and in any case we're not even sure she's going to be a match.' He sounded exasperated. Tired of trying to help his daughter and coming up against brick walls all the time.

Josh brought them up to date with what they had found out but that unfortunately Sheila had eluded them. 'I have a suggestion, but you may not like it.'

'Anything would be a good at the moment but I can't see how you can help if we can't find Sheila,' Graham commented rather dryly.

Josh could understand his frustration but ploughed on with his idea. 'I was wondering how you felt about publicity. A story about Lily in the newspaper.' Graham opened his mouth to protest but Josh held up his hand. 'Let me finish with my idea and then we can discuss it.'

The other man appeared hesitant but agreed.

'I know you're not happy about publicity. I remember Allison saying that at our first interview, but I think Lily's story needs to be told. Just to highlight the fact that donors are needed. Don't mention Sheila if you don't want to. In fact, it might be a good idea if you didn't. After all, she most likely won't be a match like the rest of your wife's family. Perhaps just a mention that all the family have been tested and now you're looking further afield. It would help attracting more people to the donor bank.'

Graham looked over at his wife and then his daughter who was so engrossed in her colouring book she was oblivious to the conversation.

'I'm not sure . . . we didn't want to put extra pressure on Lily. All the fuss it would create. You know what the press are like. It could get out of hand.'

'Yes, it could,' Josh agreed. 'But not if

it's handled sensitively. I know someone, a reporter who works for the local paper. I'm sure he would work with you and not print anything unless you agreed to every word. He may even get a small piece in the national papers, and hopefully Sheila will see it and get in touch'

Graham turned to his wife. 'What do you think, love?'

Allison bit down on her bottom lip. 'I suppose we could give it a try. What have we got to lose? We have to do something.' She looked at her daughter then brushed a tear from her eye. 'Anything we can do at this stage would be helpful.'

'OK. We'll go ahead, but we need to give full approval to the article. Possibly go with the donor problem and just a tiny bit about Lily.'

Josh was relieved, his idea was going better than he imagined. 'I'll get onto it straight away. If you don't mind I'll make the call while I'm here.'

He stood up and walked out of the room.

Megan looked at Allison, and a tear

rolled down the other woman's cheek. She reached out and squeezed her hand. 'It's going to be alright. Josh knows what he's doing.'

Allison reached for a tissue and wiped her eyes. 'Can I ask you one thing?'

'Of course, anything.'

'Would you not give up looking for my aunt? I know it's silly and we've said all along that she can't possibly help, but I've just got this feeling . . .'

The poor woman had so much faith in her belief that Megan could only agree.

'Of course. I only hope that we can find her but I have to warn you that at the moment it isn't looking good. For some reason she just doesn't want to be found, but I promise you we won't give up until you tell us to stop.'

Allison looked relieved. 'Thank you.'

'All set?' Josh said as he stepped back into the room. He handed Graham a piece of paper with the name of the journalist on it. 'Let us know how you get on and let's hope it helps.'

'Allison wants us to keep looking for

her aunt and I've said we would,' Megan said, as they drove off.

'Not sure where we go from here. Also do you think they can keep affording to pay us? I mean I'm a generous soul and we can keep the costs down as much as possible, but unfortunately, we're not in a position to do the work for free.'

'Allison told me they have a little money put by to cover the search for a few more months so we're not to worry about it.'

'OK, but we scale it down. No rushing about all over the countryside unless we have a definite lead — OK?'

'OK.' She sat back in her seat and sighed.

The whole thing was draining. All she could see was a little girl with dark circles under her eyes who should be playing in the sunlight and laughing with her friends, not stuck inside afraid to catch any infections and waiting for something good to happen to her.

Megan's mobile rang, looking at the screen she noticed it was her mother. She frowned. It was unusual for her mother to ring during the day. She usually left it until the evening so that they could have a long chat.

'Hi Mum.'

'I've been thinking about visiting you this weekend,' Joyce said, getting straight to the point as always, 'Is it convenient, or are will you be busy sleuthing?'

Megan chuckled at her mother's choice of words. 'We're purely a Monday to Friday business,' she clarified, 'Unless there happens to be an emergency and that hasn't happened as yet. Please come, I can't wait to see you and show you around my little flat, although don't expect too much, there's been no time to decorate.'

'Uncle Ronald's taste not the same as yours, I take it?'

Megan heard her mother chuckle. 'You could say that. How about we go window shopping for some ideas while you're visiting? You have a much better eye for décor than me.'

'Sounds great. Look, I won't keep

you chatting any longer. I'll see you on Saturday.'

'OK, bye.' She put down her mobile and turned to Josh. 'Looks like I'm going to have a busy weekend.'

'You miss her?'

'I know she's only a phone call away but we're very close ever since my father died. Talking on the phone isn't the same as her being next to me in person.'

Josh could only agree. He knew what it was like. His father was his best friend and he missed him like crazy. He loved his mum but it wasn't the same as talking man to man.

Megan chatted on. 'My mother never stops, she'll be dragging me from one shop to another, chattering along the way.' She laughed. 'By the time she goes home I'll be exhausted but I wouldn't have it any other way.'

'She sounds quite a character.'

'Oh she's that alright, but I love her to bits.

Oh,' she said, putting a hand to her mouth, 'How about if we invited your mum on our shopping trip. That is if she doesn't mind accompanying a human dynamo.'

It sounded like a good idea. 'I'll ask her and let you know.'

'Fancy something to eat?' Megan asked as they pulled up outside the office. 'I'm going to pop around to Sarah's.'

'Ham and cheese sandwich for me.'

He pulled out his wallet but she put up her hand. 'My treat.'

'Oh well, in that case I'll have a blueberry muffin as well,' he teased.

'Greedy!' she said, laughing. She stepped out of the car and headed off down the street.

Josh watched her as she hurried along the pavement, her shoulder length hair bounced along with her steps.

He smiled to himself as he pushed open the office door. He was fast realising that Megan was becoming an asset not only to the business but in his personal life as well. She'd taken his mother under her wing and with gentle persuasion brought her out of her depression, something that Josh would ever be grateful for.

He heard the phone ringing and quickly walked into the office to answer it.

'Mr Rayne, Robert Blackstone. I need you to step up the investigation.'

Robert Blackstone approached Josh just after Ronnie died. He was concerned about the amount of construction work he was losing to a competitor. It started off just a couple of small jobs that he could afford to lose but now larger contracts were being lost and he couldn't understand why long standing customers were going to another firm.

When he enquired about the loss of work he was informed that he was too expensive which he didn't believe for one moment, his rates were not over the top. Someone was undercutting him and he was sure that someone in his own organisation was feeding information to the opposition.

'I've done some preliminary work,'

Josh said now, 'But I haven't found anything. I've checked the staff who gather the costings of materials and they all pan out.'

'I think it's time to spread out your investigation. I'm certain it's someone in my offices and I need you to find whoever is responsible. I'm quoting for a big contract which I can't afford to lose and time is running out. I need to find the culprit within the next two weeks. If Cuthbert Builders get this next contract I might as well give up.'

Josh couldn't blame him but two weeks didn't leave him much time to do a thorough investigation, but he didn't tell Robert Blackstone that. He was a client he couldn't afford to lose. He also knew that there was no love lost between Robert Blackstone and Charles Cuthbert. Both men disliked each other intensely according to his client and it did appear that Cuthbert Builders were winning all the bids.

'Leave it with me,' Josh said, 'You'll have your culprit within the next two weeks.'

He crossed his fingers as he said the words. He wasn't sure he could make any promises but he'd do his best.

216

15

Josh was expecting an older version of Megan when he strode into her flat, not the fiery redhead who walked up to him, green eyes blazing and prodded a finger into his chest.

'So you're the man who upset my daughter,' Joyce Walters said staring him down.

'Mum!' Megan exclaimed looking horrified.

She turned to her daughter. 'Sorry, Megan but it's been festering inside of me since you told me about your first meeting with this young man.' She held out her hand to Josh. 'No hard feelings young man. We can now move on.'

He heard a giggle from behind him and looked around to see his mother with a genuine smile on her face before taking hold of Joyce's hand. He wasn't sure what to make of the woman in front of him although he now knew where

Megan got her fire from.

'I'm glad someone can put him in his place,' Marie said moving around her son and introducing herself to Joyce.

Josh looked over at Megan and shook his head, a smile played on her lips before mouthing sorry.

He walked over to her out of hearing of both mothers. Joyce seemed to have taken over the conversation and settled Marie next to her on the sofa and was chatting away.

'At least she likes my mother,' Josh said, his tone dry.

'Oh, she likes you alright,' Megan said an amused look on her face. 'If she didn't she'd have prodded you with two fingers!'

Josh looked at her as though she was joking but even with the twinkle in her eye he knew that she was serious. 'Thank goodness for that,' he said, wiping away the non-existent sweat from his forehead.

Megan looked over at the two older woman. Joyce was talking about her favourite subject — cruising and her next planned trip.

'Have you ever seen the northern lights?' Joyce asked. Marie shook her head. 'Oh you must, a magnificent sight, and the fjords are a sight to see.'

'She didn't want to come,' Josh told Megan, looking over at his mother. 'I promised if she didn't feel comfortable I'd take her straight home.' He chuckled. 'Looks as though her doubts have swiftly disappeared they seem to be getting on like a house on fire.'

'Don't worry, my mother will make her feel as though they've known each other for years.'

Suddenly Joyce sprang to her feet. 'Right, let's get this shopping expedition under way. I can't stand looking at this dreadful décor for a minute longer! I can't imagine what Uncle Ronnie was thinking. There's just so much pattern, and the colour scheme!' She shuddered as her eyes wondered around the room.

Megan agreed, the room was full of patterned wallpaper, curtains and carpet with a burgundy and cream colour scheme making the room appear far too busy. She much preferred a lighter colour scheme and up until now closed her eyes to the heavy décor.

'I believe one of Ronnie's girlfriends was into decorating. He gave her a free hand to do whatever she liked,' Josh said.

'It looks like the lounge of a 1980's pub,' Joyce said, shuddering once more. She grabbed her coat. 'Come on, ladies. No time to linger we need to see what ideas we can come up with to turn this place into something comfortable to the eye.' She hustled Marie to her feet and headed towards the door.

Megan grabbed her own coat. 'We'll see you later,' she said to Josh who'd told her that he was going to work in the office for the day.

'Anything interesting?' she'd asked but he'd shook his head.

He wanted to check on the staff at Blackstone Construction. He was now in possession of a full list of those who worked at the head office and wanted to see if anything or anyone stood out. Waving the three woman off he headed back into the office and pulled out the file and began the task of going through as many members of staff that he could with the hours he had available.

He should really mention the job to Megan but he wanted her to concentrate on helping him with finding Sheila White before involving her in another case.

He decided to start with Megan's ex.

He pulled out a sheet of paper that Robert Blackstone had provided with all the information he could provide on each employee. The file contained a picture of each member of staff. Josh studied the photograph of Marcus. He was a handsome chap with blond hair, blue eyes and what, in Josh's opinion, was a weak chin. Josh looked at his eyes again, they didn't look directly into the camera as though he had something to hide. Did he?

He brushed that notion aside and continued reading. Marcus had worked for the firm for the last four years in the sales department. There was nothing interesting about his job. As far as Josh could see he didn't have access to any vital information that would help any competitor. His next of kin was his mother, although looking at the information he had moved out of the parental home two years previous into his own flat.

Josh wondered where he got the money from, certainly not from the amount Blackstone Construction paid him when he noted his salary. Maybe he was a good saver? Something worth checking out — he made a note in the file. Perhaps he would ask Megan about her ex after all.

He worked through some of the other employees but couldn't find anything that stood out as out of the ordinary but then again if there was someone selling secrets they would be clever enough not to bring attention to themselves.

After a couple of hours he pushed away the files and scrubbed a hand of over his face and stretched his back. He'd sat down for far too long and his stomach was rumbling. He checked his watch. It was well past lunchtime and he decided to go in search of some food. He reached for his jacket and headed off to Sarah's café to see what sandwiches were on offer.

'Cheese and pickle or beef salad?' she asked as he came to the front of the lunchtime queue. He decided on beef and a coffee.

'Once this rush if over I'll have time for a chat,' she promised as she handed over his order.

He looked around for somewhere to sit. A couple were just leaving and he headed for the table in the corner. Settling himself down he bit into the sandwich, savouring the taste of the beef and the slather of horseradish sauce that accompanied it before taking a sip of the hot coffee, his taste buds responding to the flavours.

He looked around the café and was surprised to see the man who'd held his attention not an hour before. Marcus Rowland. What was he doing here? He seemed to be popping up everywhere at the moment, but didn't Megan say he had a friend who lived nearby? If that was the case why was he sitting here on his own? He took another bite of his sandwich and considered the question.

'Penny for them.'

He looked up to see Sarah standing in front of him. 'Not worth that much,' he said as she pulled out the chair opposite him and sat down.

'What's so interesting that you were staring at something over the other side of the room?'

'Megan's ex.'

'Where?' Sarah knew a little about the ex but not much.

'By the window. Fair hair, black jacket.'

Sarah turned her head, casually scanning the room so as not the make out that she was picking out Marcus in particular.

'Problem?' she asked.

Josh frowned. 'I'm not sure. He seems to be popping up every five minutes.

Megan has already seen him twice in a short space of time and now he's in the area again.'

Sarah turned a little pale. 'You don't think he wants her back, do you?'

Josh shook his head. 'From what I gather the relationship is well and truly over. Has he been in here before?'

Sarah considered it for a moment. 'I don't remember seeing him, but then again, I get a lot of passers-by. I only remember my regulars, but now you've pointed him out I'll keep an eye out.'

'Thanks. I don't want her hurt again.'

Sarah studied him for a moment.

'What?' he said, as she raised her eyebrow.

'You like her,' she stated, smiling at him.

'Of course I like her,' he said wondering where this was going.

'I mean more than just a work colleague.'

He did but he wasn't going to admit that to Sarah or she would tease him mercilessly if she knew she was right.

'She's a friend, nothing more, stop imagining things,' he said, trying to brush off the idea.

'If you say so.' The look she gave him told him he hadn't been successful in his denial.

Sarah pushed her chair back and stood up. 'You've been without a girlfriend for far too long, Josh. It's about time you did something about it.'

'I've got enough on my plate without worrying about getting a girlfriend,' he said scowling.

Sarah chuckled. 'If you say so,' she said as she picked up his empty plate and coffee cup and headed towards the counter.

His eyes drifted towards Marcus again. He was getting up from his table. Josh wondered if he should follow him and see where he was going but decided against it. He was probably worrying for nothing.

* * *

'I'm exhausted!' Megan said later that evening. She propped her feet up on a footstool and closed her eyes wishing she could have a nap but knowing her mother was still as energetic as she was first thing in the morning.

Joyce Walters had certainly been on a mission during the day, dragging both her and Marie through every shop she could think of obtaining samples of materials, wallpaper and paint until the other two women began to protest and she finally decided she was satisfied with the shopping trip.

'So what do you think?' her mother said pointing to all the samples scattered on the coffee table in front of them. She sat up and began working through the samples putting selections together to see which worked better.

Megan reluctantly opened her eyes and viewed the colour schemes. 'The blue and cream,' she decided after a moment.

'Good choice, that's what I would go for.' She sat back and sighed and they shared a comfortable silence.

'So what do you think of Josh?' Megan asked after a moment although she'd assured Josh that her mother liked him, Joyce hadn't confirmed it.

Joyce turned to her daughter. 'Good looking, hard worker and takes care of his mother, what's not to like? To answer your question, yes, I like him, and I think you like him as well.'

'I've got used to him. We've begun to work well together after a few mishaps on my part.'

She'd told her mother about the episode outside the hotel.

'I didn't mean your working relationship, although that is of course an important factor. I mean you like him in a personal way.'

Megan sighed. 'You see too much, Mum. Yes I do like him but I doubt it will go anywhere. He's too busy trying to build the business to have a girlfriend.'

'Hmm, I'm not too sure about that.'

Thinking about relationships reminded Megan of Marcus. 'I forgot to tell you, I saw I saw Marcus again.'

'Again. Here in Keatbury?'

'Yes. He was in the same restaurant as me.

He was with another man, most likely his friend.' She laughed. 'Funny bumping into him twice. Anyone would think he was following me.'

'He isn't, is he?' her mother asked frowning.

'Not at all. It's just a coincidence,' Megan said throwing the idea away. It was nonsense, why would Marcus follow her, they'd both moved on?

'Yes, that must be it,' her mother said before the conversation turned to her mother's next visit and the subject of Marcus was forgotten.

16

Josh had just finished reading the article about Lily in the local paper when Megan walked into the office. 'I need to talk to you about a case,' he said. So far the phone was silent with no one offering information so they could go no further with their search. 'Blackstone Construction.' He tapped the file on his desk with his forefinger.

'The company my ex works for?' she asked.

He nodded and opened the file.

'Robert Blackstone thinks someone in his company is passing information to a competitor. He's been losing contracts on a regular basis over the last couple of years.'

'He's certain there's a leak?'

'He is and he wants us to find it. I haven't mentioned it to you before because he wanted me to hold off until the next big contract came up and he was ready to submit his price. That's coming up in a couple of weeks and he now wants me to step up and find the culprit.'

'Any ideas?' 'I have my suspicions,' he admitted. 'I was wondering . . .'

The office door opened interrupting him before he could mention his suspicion about Marcus Rowland. He looked over to see Anne and Julie Nelson standing in the doorway, both women appeared nervous.

'Hello, ladies.' He looked over at Megan wondering if she knew anything about the visit. She looked as much surprised as he was.

Megan offered them a seat.

'What can we do for you?' she asked as they settled themselves down. Anne delved into her large handbag and pulled out a newspaper. She looked over at her sister for assurance. Julie nodded her approval.

'It's about this,' she said, holding up the newspaper and tapping an article on the page. Megan and Josh glanced at the paper. The article was about Lily and the donor appeal.

'We didn't know, you see.' Anne bit down on her bottom lip and Megan noticed her hand shaking slightly. 'If we'd have known we would have told you sooner, but we'd made a promise and you should never break a promise, should you?'

Megan was bemused. What on earth were they talking about? 'No, you shouldn't break a promise, not unless there's no other option.'

'When we read the article about poor Lily Frampton we knew we should come and see you. If only we'd known before.' Both women looked upset and about ready to burst into tears.

Megan pulled her chair closer to the two women. 'How about you tell us what all this is about. Take a deep breath and just go with the flow as they say,' she said gently.

Both women gave her a weak smile.

Anne took a deep breath. 'When we read about poor Lily and her struggle to find a donor and that no family member matched we knew then why you'd come to us asking questions about dear Sheila, but we'd promised you see.'

'Sorry, what do you mean you promised?' Josh asked, looking puzzled.

Anne said, 'We know where Sheila is.'

Josh leaned forward at his desk. 'You do? But why on earth didn't you say?' He tried not to raise his voice but failed and the two woman pulled out hankies and dabbed at their eyes.

'Josh,' Megan admonished, shaking her head.

'Sorry,' he said, gentling his voice. 'Care to start from the beginning, ladies?'

Anne hesitated for a moment but a nudge from her sister encouraged her to start her story.

'Sheila told us that she was leaving all those years ago. We wanted her to stay but she was determined. Anyway at the same time she sent her parents that postcard we received one as well but on ours Sheila wrote her address. We began a correspondence. Of course, we didn't want our parents to know so we got one of those post office boxes and the corre-spondence sent there.'

How very inventive of them. Megan was surprised they'd come up with such an idea.

'Over the years Sheila would tell us her news,' Anne continued. 'She became our pen pal, I suppose you'd call it. We laughed when she told us she now called herself Natalie, it was so like her.' Anne glanced at Julie who laughed. 'And then when she became a fortune teller it sounded so glamorous and exciting.'

'Did you never think to tell her par-ents where she was? They must have been worried.'

'We did think about it at first but they'd already gone to Pendry Cove and she'd already left.

When they returned they decided not to look for her in the hope that she would return of her own accord. Of course, that never happened and over the years her name was mentioned less and less. We got the impression that her parents accepted she'd started a new life and every time we broached the subject of her getting in touch with her parents, she begged us not to tell.'

Julie reached over and clutched her sister's hand before picking up the story. 'We were surprised when she left the fair and the fortune telling but by then she'd met her husband.'

'Brian Mathers.'

'Oh, you know about him?'

'We are detectives,' Josh said with a smile.

'Yes, yes, of course you are.'

'So you know that she reverted to Sheila and married Brian.'

'Yes, that much we've found out but they've moved from their last address and are now travelling along the canals of England. We have no idea where they are.'

Anne pulled out a postcard from her handbag. 'We received this a couple of weeks ago. Sheila and Brian are moored here and are staying for six weeks.' She held out the card to Megan who read it before passing it to Josh.

At last they'd found Sheila!

'Thank you, ladies, 'Josh said, writing down the address in his notebook. 'You've done the right thing.'

'We just hope it will help poor Lily.'

'Let's hope so too, although we can't guarantee it,' he said handing back the postcard.

The two ladies stood up ready to go, but Josh stopped them.

'Just one thing. Can I ask you not to get in touch with Sheila and tell her we're looking for her? She could do another runner, you see.'

The question was silently passed between the two women before they both agreed.

'Once again, thank you, ladies. I think it's time that Sheila stopped running and is reunited with her family.'

'She's missed so much,' said Julie, 'Even though we kept her up to date with any family news. We told her about her sister passing, you know. Pleaded with her to come to the funeral but she said it was best left alone, although she did slip back a couple of days later and laid some flowers on the grave then slipped away again.'

How sad, pondered Megan that she couldn't bring herself to call on her niece while she was home and they could have grieved together. Such a waste of time.

The two women left the office apologising every second until Megan assured them they would be in touch after they'd talked to Sheila.

She turned to Josh who had a smile as wide as the office on his face. 'We've found her Megan!'

He grabbed hold of her waist and lifted her off the ground before swinging her around.

Megan laughed. 'Put me down, idiot!' she said tapping him on the shoulder.

He lowered her down and looked at her, his eyes sparkling, and promptly kissed her!

Megan was expecting a quick peck but it began to turn into something stronger, something with meaning. Oh lord, she was in trouble. She didn't want it to end but Josh suddenly pulled away.

'Megan I . . .' he whispered.

Was he going to apologise? If he was, she wasn't sure she could handle it!

'That's OK, we both got carried away. Think nothing of it,' she said quickly not wanting to hear what he was going to say. She turned back to her desk and picked up the phone, needing to do something.

'What are you doing?' he asked, a little hurt that she didn't want to listen to him.

'Ringing the Frampton's. They'll want to know the good news.'

He reached out and took the phone from her. He noted that her hand shook a little, so she wasn't unaffected by what just happened. He decided that now was not the time to talk about what was happening between them. It could be discussed later. He let go of her hand.

'I don't think that's a good idea.'

She looked at him, puzzled. 'Why ever not?'

'Think about it, Megan. She's spent years not wanting to be found. Staying away from her family. She's made a new life for herself. Maybe she wants to keep it that way.'

'But surely she'll want to help once she knows the story. Who wouldn't?' Megan couldn't understand his reasoning.

'But what if she doesn't? We don't know her. Maybe she'll decide not to help. What would be the point of telling the Framptons? Raising their hopes and then having to tell them that she refuses to help.'

Megan realised what he said made sense. They shouldn't raise everyone's hopes until they'd spoken to the missing woman.

'I suppose you're right.'

Josh put the phone back on its cradle and looked at his watch. 'The boat's moored a couple of hours away from here. We'll go first thing in the morning.'

'Fine.' She wasn't sure what else to say.

The kiss still hung in the air between them and Josh must have sensed the same thing and she was sure he was going to say something more, but in the end decided against it. Instead he walked over to his desk and began reading something on his computer.

She decided she wasn't going to push him, after all her own emotions were upside down even more than before the kiss. Concentrate on the visit tomorrow she told herself as she began updating the records on the Sheila White case.

She was still mulling over all that occurred during the day when she sat eating her supper that evening.

The kiss, Sheila White, even Marcus came into her mind. The Blackstone case. What was Josh going to say about Marcus? They hadn't returned to the conversation after the Nelson twins left the office. She couldn't imagine what Marcus had to do with any of it. She decided to ask Josh tomorrow after they'd found Sheila White.

* * *

Josh stared into space. He was thinking about Megan which wasn't surprising, she'd been on his mind since that kiss.

The trouble was he was beginning to like it too much. He admitted his feelings towards her were changing and it shocked him. How it happened he didn't know! One minute he wanted her out of his life for good the next minute he didn't think he could live without her! He'd become used going into the office in the morning where a welcoming cup of coffee was on his desk. It wasn't just that though. She made him laugh, something he hadn't done in a long time. He was surprised how much his mother was coming out of her shell since Megan encouraged her to go the flower arranging class. She was out tonight with someone she'd met there. Gone for a drink, would you believe? His mother didn't go out for drinks! She was changing and he was glad. She'd even enjoyed the shopping expedition and chatted for hours about Joyce and was even thinking about going on a cruise. How things were changing since Megan came into his life!

He frowned, thinking about Marcus Rowland. He'd forgotten to continue the conversation about Blackstone Construction with Megan. He needed to sort that out as soon as possible, but decided to leave it until they'd met with Sheila White. Lily Frampton's health was more important and Marcus Rowland could wait for a couple of days.

17

'Have you ever been on a canal boat?' Megan asked as she settled down in the passenger seat of Josh's car the next morning. Once again she decided not to mention the kiss, thinking that it was just a sudden decision on Josh's part and he probably regretted it. She wished she could have done the same, but the memory lingered.

'Not me,' Josh said, shuddering at the idea. It wasn't his idea of a holiday. 'Had a friend who took his family on one of those ring things once.'

'Ring things?' She looked puzzled.

Josh looked across at her for the first time since she settled in the car. 'I think that's what you call them. Going from lock to lock in a circle.

'Goodness, you learn something every day.' 'My friend was all for it until he realised that you did all that stuff with the locks. You know, getting off the boat and turning handles to higher or lower the water level. I don't remember all the details but the next time I saw him he grumbled about how much work it was and that they didn't have a relaxing holiday at all.' He chuckled. 'The following year he booked a fortnight in Spain. A sunny beach and no work.'

'Sounds like fun to me. Are you an energetic person on holiday or do you to take in the rays?'

Josh shrugged. 'I'm not sure what I am, to be honest. It's been such a long time since I've been on holiday. But thinking about it I'm probably a bit of both. I mean I don't mind relaxing for the first few days but it would get boring just laying on a beach and doing nothing for fourteen days. I think I'd like to explore whatever places I visit. You know, get the feel of the area.'

Megan agreed. That sounded like her kind of holiday. The last time she'd been away she went with a walking group on a rambling holiday around France. It was great to see places that were off the tourist route and the culture was much more interesting.

'Right, we'd better get on our way. Let's just hope we're not on another wild goose chase and they're still there when we turn up.'

'The sisters seemed pretty sure they would.'

Josh said nothing, turning on the engine and moving swiftly into the traffic.

The rain from the night before had disappeared and the morning brought cloudless skies and warm weather. Ideal for holidaying on the canals.

'I still can't get over the sisters being in contact with Sheila all these years and keeping it to themselves. You know, I thought there was something odd when we went to see them.'

'What do you mean, odd?'

'Oh I don't know. The way they looked at each other as though they were communicating between themselves in a silent conversation.'

Josh glanced at her for a moment before concentrating on the road. 'Like telepathy?'

'Yes, something like that. Aren't twins supposed to have the ability?'

'I have heard of it but you could be right about the twins. Even yesterday they kept turning to each other as though they were seeking approval before telling us what we wanted to know.'

'Lucky us that they both silently agreed to help,' he said wryly.

Conversation turned to their hopes of at last finding Sheila and in what seemed a short space of time they reached their destination.

There were a few boats moored alongside the canal. Some new, some old, some brightly painted and some more muted in colour. As they stepped out of the car Megan couldn't help but admire the brightly coloured ones, reds and blues were the main colours with brightly coloured decoration on the sides. Some with flowers, some with patterns. There was even a garden growing on the roof of one of the canal boats.

There were several couples sitting on

the decks, drinking tea and enjoying the sunshine. It seemed that they'd found a life that suited them.

The *Second Chance* was a good distance from the lock, tucked away beyond a bend in the canal. Painted black with a gold trim it blended in with the other boats moored along the canal. A couple were outside, sitting at a picnic table playing cards.

'That looks like her,' said Megan. Although she'd aged there was a resemblance to the photograph they'd been given. Her husband was in his sixties with receding grey hair. Megan guessed he was used to manual work from his trim figure, there didn't seem to be an ounce of fat on the man.

'Good morning,' Josh called out as they approached. 'You don't happen to be Mr and Mrs Mathers, do you?'

'That we are,' Brian Mathers said 'Are you from the lock keepers cottage? Is there a problem?'

'No, nothing like that. I'm Josh Rayne and this is my partner Megan Walters.'

Josh hoped by introducing Megan as his partner they would think of them as in a romantic relationship and would be more relaxed when they sprang the surprise that they were, in fact, looking for Sheila.

'Pleased to meet you. I'm Brian and this is my wife, Sheila,' he said tilting his head towards his wife who gave them a wide smile. 'So if there isn't a problem, what can we do for you?'

Josh moved a little nearer the boat. 'Actually we're private detectives and we're looking for Sheila White, which I believe is you, Mrs Mathers.'

The smile disappeared from Sheila's face and her husband stood up and walked behind his wife and laid his hands on her shoulders. There was a coldness about his look.

'What do you want? She's done nothing wrong.' Brian Mathers tone turned from friendly to frosty in an instant.

Josh raised a hand. 'No, no, you're not in any kind of trouble, Mrs Mathers,' he was quick to assure her. 'But your family have been looking for you.'

'I haven't got any family,' Sheila said, not denying who she was. 'They're all gone.'

'Not quite, you have a niece, and she's looking for you.'

'How did you find me?' she asked, ignoring the remark he'd made about having a niece.

'Julie and Anne Nelson. They came forward when they read the article.'

'What article?'

Megan pulled out a news cutting from her bag. 'I think this will explain better than we can.' They'd decided to bring the newspaper article with them in the hope that it would encourage Sheila to come home.

'What is it?' The woman asked looking at Megan with suspicion.

'Look, can we come on board? It's a bit difficult to talk — or rather shout — from this distance.'

Brian Mathers glanced at his wife who consented. 'Come aboard,' he said.

Josh hopped onto the desk with ease

before holding out his hand to assist Megan.

'Here you are,' Megan said handing over the newspaper article to Sheila.

She popped on a pair of glasses and began reading, her husband standing behind her doing the same. Megan watched as a stream of emotions crossed the woman's face. The article obviously affected her. She looked up and took off her glasses. 'That poor child, but I don't see how I can help.'

Josh explained the situation. 'Of course, it doesn't mean you would definitely be a match, but Allison wants to give it a try.'

Sheila looked at her husband unsure what to do or say. He just squeezed her shoulder giving her some kind of reassurance.

The woman gave a big sigh. 'It's been such a long time since I've seen any of my family. I was stupid running away like I did. Such big ideas that never came to anything, and as for the row with my sister . . .' She looked over at Megan.

'I suppose you know the story.' Megan nodded and Sheila continued. 'Do you know, I can't even remember what that boy looked like? It was stupid but I was young and thought I'd been hard done by.'

'You did a good job of hiding away. Luckily you sent that postcard to your parents so we were given a starting point,' Josh said. 'It's just taken us a while to chase you down.'

Sheila gave a slight smile. 'I was rather good at disappearing, wasn't I? So that's how you got onto my trail. I needed to send my parents something. They would have been worried but I didn't want them to find me and I knew they would come looking. Fancy them keeping that card for all these years.'

'We followed your trail from Pendry Cove and your old boyfriend, to the fair and Madam Mystery, to being married to Brian, I have to admit that you've been on quite an adventure.'

Sheila smiled reaching up, clasping Brian's hand which lay on her shoulder. 'My gallivanting stopped once I met this man.'

Brian kissed the top of his wife's head and smiled down at her. 'Best meeting of my life.'

'Why the name change?' Megan asked. 'I mean, I suppose I can understand you changing your name initially to Natalie to try and hide but you've changed it back again.'

Sheila fingered the playing cards on the table. 'When I was young I never liked my name. Wanted something more glamorous and settled on Natalie.' She gave a wry smile. 'My next name change, Madam Mystery, came with the job.'

Megan liked her own name but could see why some people didn't so she just accepted Sheila's explanation.

Sheila looked up at her husband. 'When I met Brian I explained to him and he said why not change it back again. It seemed a good idea.' She laughed. 'I must confess Sheila seems to suit me much better.

'OK, Sheila,' said Josh. It didn't matter what she was called now, all that mattered was that they'd found her. Now he needed to know if she was willing to meet up with the only other family she had left and take the test. 'So what can I tell Allison? Are you willing to meet up and discuss the possibility of helping the family out?'

'Of course I want to help,' Sheila said not hesitating to think about it. 'As you say I'm most likely not a match like the rest of the family but if there is a possibility that I am, I'll do all I can for this little girl.'

'Your great-niece,' Megan reminded her.

'Why, yes, of course. I've never been called auntie before. Brian is an only child and we have none of our own. A look of sadness crossed her features. 'Never been that lucky.' She looked at Josh. 'Could you ring her now and tell her that I've been found and I'm willing to meet and help in whatever way is possible?'

'Certainly,' He pulled out his mobile and moved away from the couple and dialled Allison with the news. 'She wants to talk to you,' Josh said a few minutes later holding out his mobile to Sheila. Her hands shook as she took the mobile from him.

'Let's give them some privacy,' Megan said going to Josh's side linking her arm with his and giving a gentle tug.

They moved to the bow of the boat and watched a family of ducks swim past. 'We've done it.' Megan whispered. She turned back for a moment and could see that there was a genuine smile on Sheila's face. It looked as though things were going well.

'Been quite a journey, hasn't it?'

It certainly had and one she wouldn't have missed for the world. She wondered if all cases ended so happily. She doubted it.

'Do you mind if we come back with you?' Brian Mathers said approaching them. 'Sheila wants to meet her niece and her family as soon as possible.' He turned to look at his wife. 'Do you know I've never seen her so happy. She's never talked much about her family after she first explained why she'd run away. A couple of times I tried to persuade her to make contact but she always refused.' He grinned. 'My wife can be very stubborn when she wants to be. So is it OK? Coming back with you I mean.'

'Of course?' Josh assured him. 'Are you alright leaving your boat here for a couple of days?'

'It'll be fine. We planned on staying for a while anyway. I'll just let the lock keeper know so he can keep an eye on the boat.'

Sheila finished her conversation and joined them. 'Allison invited us to stay the night, I'll go and pack a few things,' she said when Brian told her they would be going back with the other couple. She turned to go then turned back. 'Thanks for finding me,' she said before disappearing through an open set of doors that descended into the living quarters of the boat.

★ ★ ★

The journey back was full of chatter from Sheila who, once she accepted that she had family, couldn't stop asking questions. Josh and Megan filled the other couple in with what details they knew but it wasn't a lot.

'Of course the twins told me a lot of what was going on over the years but I still don't understand why they didn't mention Lily's illness.'

'Because they didn't know,' Megan said. 'Allison and her husband didn't want a lot of publicity about Lily's illness. They thought there would be a match on one of Graham's side of the family but as we've already mentioned that didn't happen. Hence the search for you. It was only when Josh suggested that a bit of publicity might help with the donor bank that they read about Lilly and saw the urgency of the matter. Thank goodness they came forward, or I don't think we would have ever found you.'

Sheila chuckled. 'I have happy memories of the three of us and some of the things we got up to. You know I'm not surprised they never married. They were inseparable even when they were young and were lucky that they knew what each other was thinking.' She went on to tell Megan some of the antics they got up to and as the journey came to an end they were all laughing, which pleased Megan as she wanted Sheila to be relaxed when she met her family after so long.

The laughter stopped as Josh pulled up outside the Frampton's home, and Megan could feel the tension in the car. Sheila was nervous and Brian looked anxious for his wife

Megan reached out and squeezed the older woman's hand. 'It's going to be fine.'

Sheila gave her a weak smile and looked out of the car window. Megan followed her gaze. Allison must have been watching for the car to arrive because she was walking down the path, a broad smile on her face.

'Come on, out you get,' Megan said to the couple. She opened her own door ready to step out but Josh put a hand on her arm.

'Let's leave them to it. We'll get in touch in a couple of hours once they've talked things over. This is a private family time.'

He was right, it would be an intrusion. She closed the car door and watched as Sheila and Brian walked up the path. There was no hesitation on Allison's part as she threw her arms around her aunt hugging her tight. It looked as though everything was going to work out just fine.

She wound her window down. 'We'll be in touch,' she called to Allison who waved and mouthed *thank you*. Megan sat back in the passenger seat and breathed a sigh of relief. Her first case wrapped up. She just hoped that it would be a happy ending for Lily.

18

Josh needed to stretch his legs. Sitting in his car for the last two hours waiting for Marcus Rowland to leave his flat wasn't happening. The man had been on his mind for the last few days and now that Sheila White was found he could concentrate on the Blackstone case.

There was something not right about Megan's ex-boyfriend. Why did he keep turning up? If he wanted Megan back why hadn't he made any kind of move? It didn't make sense, but he was going to find out and then he'd talk to Megan. He'd not mentioned his concerns to her and she wouldn't be happy about him keeping secrets from her but he felt justified. What was the point in saying anything if there was nothing to worry about?

He didn't think that was the case as soon as he'd pulled up outside the block of flats. How did a man who worked in a sales office afford a newly built flat? He immediately checked on the prices of such flats on his mobile and was surprised to see the high cost of them. Marcus lived at number four with each flat having its own designated parking space — parked in number 4 was a flashy sports car and not an old model at that. So far nothing was adding up.

Josh shuffled in his seat. He'd seen nothing of Marcus, but that wasn't surprising as it was ten o'clock on a Sunday morning and any self-respecting person would be eating a leisurely breakfast and reading the Sunday papers.

He took a sip of the coffee he'd bought two hours ago, grimacing when he realised it was now cold. He put it back in the cup holder wishing he'd brought a flask of the hot liquid. Sometimes he hated doing surveillance but it was the only way to gain the information he needed.

Another hour passed and he was about to give up when he saw a car approaching and turn into the car park before pulling into one of the visitors parking spots. The driver's door stayed shut for a moment and then a man he recognised climbed out — Terry Cuthbert from Cuthbert Builders.

The entrance door to the flats opened and he wasn't at all surprised to see Marcus Rowland appear and walk over to the car. The two men shook hands and Marcus pressed something into Terry's hand. Josh grabbed his mobile and took a picture for evidence. The two men spoke for a few minutes before Terry climbed back into his car. Marcus watched the car disappear out of sight before returning inside. The whole episode was over within ten minutes.

This confirmed Josh's suspicions. Marcus was passing information onto Blackstone's competitors. He looked at the photograph he'd taken. Unfortunately, he was too late to catch whatever had passed between the two men. He only hoped it was enough to help Robert Blackstone.

As he drove off the curtains twitched at No 4. Marcus was speaking into his mobile as he watched Josh disappeared from view.

★ ★ ★

'What's wrong?' Megan asked looking at Josh as she walked into the office on Monday morning, He was at his desk drumming his fingers on the top, a deep frown creasing his brow.

For the remainder of Sunday Josh had wondered how he was going to tell Megan about his suspicions and decided the direct approach would be the best, but he doubted she would like the fact that he hadn't told her what he was up to.

'It's about your ex.'

She frowned. 'Marcus. What about him?'

'He keeps popping up. He was in the café the other day. I wondered if he was following you.'

Megan considered it for a moment. 'I must admit when I bumped into him a couple of times I did wonder, but I'm sure it's just a coincidence. He hasn't bothered me and apart from the first time hasn't even spoken to me. I'm sure you're overreacting.'

'You're sure you don't want to get back with him?' Josh held his breath hoping she'd say no. Neither mentioned the last time they'd kissed. Josh wanted to check out Marcus first. He wasn't sure why Megan hadn't brought up the subject.

'Fat chance of that. This girl is not interested,' she scoffed, wondering why Josh was asking her about her ex. Surely they'd moved on from her past relationship. Her thoughts were running along the same lines as his. That last kiss. She was hoping he'd mention it but his lips were sealed on the subject and she didn't feel confident enough to mention it herself.

They gazed at each other for a moment and she was sure she saw relief in his eyes. His tense shoulders began to relax as if he was pleased with her response.

'Pleased to hear it.' He scrubbed a hand over his chin. 'Anyway as he works for Blackstone's and as I was asked to check out all the employees I decided to start with him.' He took a deep breath. 'So yesterday I sat outside his flat for a couple hours to see if he did anything suspicious.'

Megan's mouth opened and closed it like a goldfish before she found her voice. 'You did what? Without me? I was under the impression we'd agreed to work together.' She glared at him.

He wasn't surprised by her reaction although he wondered if she was angrier at him for going ahead with something on his own or the fact that he suspected her ex-boyfriend.

'It was a Sunday. You were visiting your mother. I didn't have anything planned. I went with my intuition.' He stared at her. 'Plus you're a little too close to the subject.'

'A little too close. What does that mean?' Her blue eyes sparkled with anger.

He stood up and walked around his desk. 'Come on Megan. Would you have believed me if I'd told you that Marcus could be the culprit?'

She swallowed down her anger and accepted that he was making a good point. 'Possibly not,' she conceded. 'So what did you find out?'

He opened a folder on his desk and plucked out a couple of photographs.

'That's Robert Blackstone,' he said as she looked at the first photograph. She recognised him as the man she'd almost bumped into outside the office one day.

'Do you recognise anyone in the other photograph?' he asked.

She gazed at the faces of three men, all smiling. She recognised one of them immediately. 'That's Marcus's friend, the one he was with the night we went to Luigi's,' she said, pointing to the youngest of the three men. Who is he?'

So that was who he as dining with. Josh recalled that he hadn't seen the other man or he would have been immediately suspicious.

'Terry Cuthbert. Works for his uncle at Cuthbert Builders, he's the man in the middle. The other man is Terry's father, he's a director of the company but has very little to do with the everyday running of the business. They're Blackstone's main competitor.' He went on to tell her about seeing the two men together and showing her the photograph he'd taken.

'I thought I knew Marcus so well. So much for me being a good judge of character.' She continued studying the photograph.

'What's wrong?' asked Josh, noticing her looking at something in particular.

She tapped her finger on the company logo under which the men were standing. 'This, I've seen it before. It was the night Marcus and I fell out. I was at his flat — we were going out and I was waiting for him. His laptop was open and I caught sight of an email he'd opened. That logo was on the top. I didn't think anything of it but he went mad when he walked into the room and saw what I was looking at. He pushed me aside and closed the message and then went on to accuse me of being nosy. We had the most terrible row about trust and it ended with me walking out.'

She was silent for a moment, it seemed that everything was falling into place. 'You know I always wondered why he seemed to have plenty of money and the sports car he drove, and then there was the flat. I commented on it once and he told me his grandmother died and left him some money. It seemed a reasonable explanation and I never queried it. Why would I?'

Josh said nothing, just let her talk.

'You know, the first time I saw him outside of this building he looked shocked to see me. He must have found out you were working for Blackstone's and come to check you out. What he didn't expect was to find me working here.'

'I think you're right. That must be why he's been turning up all the time trying to find out what we're up to.'

'Have you reported it back to Mr Blackstone?'

Josh shook his head. 'I tried to ring him first thing this morning but he's away and his secretary said he was uncontactable until tomorrow. Plus, we have a problem . . .'

'What problem?'

'Proof.'

'What do you mean? You have a photograph. That's proof, isn't it?'

'It's just a photograph of two men talking and although I'm sure Marcus passed something like a memory stick to Terry the photo doesn't show it happening.'

'So what do you suggest we do now?'

'I'm not sure. Let me talk to Robert Blackstone first. He may want to approach it differently.'

Before Megan could say anything further her mobile beeped. 'Oh bother,' she said looking at the text. 'I'd forgotten I'd invited Sarah for a girly night in tonight. A pizza and a chick flick.'

'Sounds exciting.' Josh tried to keep the dryness out of his voice.

Megan gave him a look. 'After the revelations of today, a relaxing evening with a friend is just what I need.' She stood up and grabbed her handbag. 'I'm just popping out to pick up a bottle of wine.' She gave him a stern look. 'Don't do anything until I get back.'

★ ★ ★

As Megan walked back home clutching the bottle of wine she went over the day's events. It seemed such a long time ago that they'd found Sheila White and brought her back to her niece's house. Now there was another problem to attend to. Life certainly never stopped at the detective agency. She thought of Marcus. How wrong could she have been about the man? She still couldn't believe what Josh told her about him but the more she went over the time she spent with Marcus the more she realised he did seem to live above his means. Was that what made him turn to crime? She'd a good mind to go and have it out with him, but she'd already interferred in a case without telling Josh with near disastrous results in the Swinson case.

No, it was best she left well alone until they decided what action to take.

Josh was unlocking his car when she got back.

'I just got a tip about Jimmy,' he explained as he opened the car door. 'Hopefully I won't be too long.' He looked at his watch. It was the end of the day and the light was fading. Jimmy had been spotted helping someone moving house. A large amount of furniture was being moved according to Josh's source. He'd have to be quick if he was going to catch him out once and for all. 'Got to dash,' he said, jumping into his car. 'Shouldn't be too long,' he shouted as he drove off.

* * *

Megan walked into her flat and put the bottle of white wine in the fridge. There was still another hour before the office closed. Feeling restless she decided to go back into the office and study the Blackstone case in depth. She made herself a cup of coffee and picked up the folder from Josh's desk and began reading.

The sound of the office door opening made her look up, the welcoming smile on her face disappearing and turning to one of surprise as she recognised who stood in the doorway.

'Marcus.'

'Hello, Megan. I was passing and decided I'd drop in to see where you worked.'

The tone of his voice was different and she was immediately suspicious. He stepped inside the office and began looking around the room before resting his eyes on her. The look in his eyes, it wasn't something she'd ever seen before. Sinister was the word that came to mind.

She heard a shuffling in the corridor and looked to see Terry Cuthbert appearing in the doorway.

Marcus looked over his shoulder. 'My friend Terry wanted to see where you worked, too. He might have a job for you.' His tone was sarcastic but she chose to ignore it.

'Job for me?' she said, knowing full well that Terry hadn't come to enquire about a job. She felt uncomfortable and wished Josh was here.

Marcus walked to Josh's desk and sat down, his hands resting on the desktop.

'Yes. You see he's a little concerned about someone who appears to be following him. He was so concerned that he came to me. I suggested he get a private detective to find out what the problem was. I remember you telling me about your new job so, of course, I suggested he come and see you.'

There was a smile on his face as he related his tale but it didn't reach his eyes.

Megan fumbled on her desk for her mobile but realised too late that she'd left it in her flat. She looked at the office telephone contemplating if she could make a call without the two men noticing. Instinctively she reached for it but Terry Cuthbert was too quick and moved swiftly to the phone pulling the cord from its socket.

Marcus chuckled. 'I don't think so. We wouldn't want anyone to be alerted before we finish our chat would we?'

'What do you want, Marcus? If you think I believe your cock and bull story about a job then you're sadly mistaken.' Megan kept her voice calm although her insides were churning.

'No, I didn't think you would. Why don't we wait until your boss returns and he might believe me?'

'One, he's not my boss, he's my part-ner,' she snapped, 'And two, he won't believe a word that comes out of your mouth any more than I do.'

Marcus shrugged. 'Probably not. Where is he?'

'Out. But he'll be back soon.'

'Good, then we'll wait.'

Megan didn't like the sound of that at all. She looked over at Terry who was back to standing in the doorway blocking anyone from entering. Marcus seemed comfortable and composed, too com-posed for Megan's liking.

The silence stretched out. Megan kept

quiet. What was there to say?

Marcus pulled his mobile from his pocket and became absorbed in whatever was on the screen while Terry leant against the doorframe and stared into space. An hour passed and then Megan heard the front door open. Marcus looked up and turned off his mobile and Terry straightened, putting his hand in his pocket and draw something out. She was alarmed to see it was a gun which he pointed at her, putting a finger to his mouth indicating that she should keep quiet. They were in trouble and she wasn't sure how they were going to get out of it.

19

Josh whistled as he locked his car. After months of trying to catch Jimmy Donaldson, he'd finally done it. He tapped his mobile and looked at the evidence once again — Jimmy lifting a fridge and putting it into the boot of a car. No doubt about it, the man was as fit as a fiddle.

Two cases wrapped up in a matter of days — sometimes life was good and it looked like the Blackstone case would find closure soon too. He saw lights on in the office. Megan must still be working. He felt like celebrating and hopefully she'd join him. He tossed his car keys in the air before catching them and putting them in his trouser pocket.

'I've got him!' he shouted as he pushed open the door to the office.

The smile he was wearing dropped the instant he saw Marcus Rowland sitting at his desk, with Terry Cuthbert standing behind Megan. Her face was pale — and no wonder, with a gun poking into her shoulder.

Josh clenched his fists, this was not good!

'Marcus Rowland, I believe,' he said, his voice calm and not denying he knew the man.

Marcus leant back in the chair, crossed his arms across his chest and stared at Josh before speaking. 'Oh, you know very well who I am since I'm the one you've been following.'

'I have?'

Marcus twisted his lips into a grin. 'Oh yes. I spotted you yesterday outside my home.' He paused for a moment before unfolding his arms and standing up. He moved in front of the desk looking directly at Josh. 'And I know why.'

'You do?' Josh didn't deny anything, there was little point.

Marcus smirked. 'It's a pity you've found out about my little enterprise. Unfortunately, I can't allow you to report anything back to my superiors.'

'How do you know I haven't already?'

Josh asked, hoping Marcus didn't know about him being unable to make contact with his boss.

'Oh, I know a lot. For instance, Robert Blackstone cannot be reached at the moment.

Josh raised an eyebrow.

'Oh, you want to know how I know? The same way I know the information his competitors want.' Marcus leant against the desk and pushed his hands into his trouser pockets, completely at ease with the situation. 'It helps when the woman that types the quotes thinks you're the best thing since sliced bread and will tell you anything.' He chuckled to himself. 'It's even better when she's best friends with the boss's secretary and they both like to gossip.'

So that's how he managed to get the information — so simple!

'But why, Marcus?' Megan said, speaking for the first time since Josh entered the room. 'Why did they approach you and not someone else?'

'Oh you've got it all wrong, my dear

Megan. It wasn't they who approached me, quite the opposite.' He chuckled again something that Josh wished he'd stop doing. This man was far too relaxed for his liking. 'Let's say I saw an opportunity and took it. Cuthbert's are quite happy to pay me a considerable amount of money for the information. You'd be surprised how much there is to be made from winning big contracts.'

'But how did you know about me?' Josh asked.

'Same way. Secretaries talk. I must admit I did wonder how much you knew and how close you were to finding out anything relevant. It was just my bad luck that day I came to call on you on some pretence and I bumped into Megan. Imagine my surprise when I found out about her good fortune. Of course, the fact that she saw something she shouldn't have at my flat meant that sooner or later you'd put two and two together. I did think you hadn't found out about me. I checked your office, even Megan's flat but found nothing.'

'It was you! I did wonder why the front door was open when I was certain I'd locked it. Then I got a feeling someone had been in my flat.'

'Yes, I was lucky that day, just managed to leave before you came home. By the way you need to decorate — terrible décor.'

'Stop being flippant, Marcus. It doesn't suit you,' Megan said, her eyes flashing.

'Sorry, can't help myself.' He became serious again. 'When I saw your partner outside my flat it confirmed you were onto me.'

Before Josh or Megan could say anything further Marcus's mobile beeped and he quickly glanced down and read whatever message was on the screen. 'Time to go,' he said standing up.

Terry nudged Megan in the shoulder with the barrel of the gun causing Josh to see red. There was no way he was going to allow her to be hurt. He made a move towards her but Terry pushed the gun further into her side making her wince.

'Don't even think about it,' Terry said. He grabbed hold of Megan's arm and pulled her to her feet. 'Come on, let's get this over with.'

'Sorry about that,' Marcus said pushing himself away from the desk although he didn't look sorry at all. 'Terry can be a little impatient.'

Josh ignored both men and reached for Megan's hand giving it a reassuring squeeze. He looked into her eyes and was relieved to see the fear had disappeared.

She turned to Marcus. 'Where are you taking us?' she asked as Terry pulled her to the door.

Josh was interested to know the answer to that, too. If they were going to get out of this mess he needed as much information as the two men would give them. There was no chance of escape at the moment, not with a gun being pushed into Megan's side. He could possibly take on Marcus in a one-on-one fight but Terry was another matter. He'd shoot Megan at a moment's notice, Josh didn't doubt it. No, it was best he bided his time and hopefully there would be an opportunity to turn the tables on the two men later.

'Cuthbert's are building a new office block on Drake Road. Nice and quiet at this time of night.'

Terry waved the gun at Josh indicating him to move out of the office. 'No funny business from either of you once we're outside. Any noise,' he said looking at Josh, 'And your girlfriend will be in a whole lot of pain.' Terry shoved her in front of him causing her to stumble.

'Hey, no need to be rough with her,' Josh said glaring at Terry but the man just ignored him.

'You know you're not going to get away with this,' Megan said as they walked outside. Terry nudged her in the back with his gun. 'Shut up and keep walking. The car's across the road.'

Megan looked around, it was dark and there was no one on the street to call for help although she could have sworn she saw a shadow in one of the doorways. Perhaps someone was watching.

'Drake Road office block, is that where you said you were taking us?' She raised her voice hoping if anyone was out there they would hear her.

'Keep your voice down,' Terry hissed, nudging her towards the vehicle.

'Don't try anything,' Marcus said as he shoved Josh into the passenger seat and went round to the driver's side. Terry was already sitting in the back with Megan. He turned to Josh. 'Just remember, Megan will get hurt if you doing anything stupid.'

Josh said nothing, his mind turning over wondering when he might get an opportunity to stop this madness. He didn't think Marcus was a killer but he wasn't too sure about Terry. The possibility was there and all he could think about was Megan's safety.

The drive to the half-built office block was done in silence. Josh had to admire Megan for keeping her cool — most other women would be weeping buckets by now, but she'd just kept quiet, apart from a couple of comments in the office and then when she raised voice just before getting in the car. What was that all about?

The building was deserted, the workmen all having gone home for the day. There was going to be no help there. Marcus led them into a large windowless room, Terry following behind, stationing himself at the entrance of the doorway blocking any chance of escape

Josh scanned the room. It was littered with pots of paint and shelving units ready to be assembled. There didn't seem to be anything he could use to aid their escape.

'Look Marcus, it's not too late to stop all this,' Megan said. She hoped he would see reason for old times' sake — after all, they'd once been close. 'You're not going to go to prison for this, probably a fine and the loss of your job. But getting rid of us isn't going to help your cause.'

Marcus shook his head. 'Sorry Megan, but it's gone too far. You're right, I doubt I would get a prison sentence if it was just the undercutting of prices but I'm afraid it goes much deeper than that. Terry and I saw another gap in the market, buying extra materials, charging the customer and then selling them to African countries. You'd be surprised at the level of demand in some of these countries.

'And Charles Cuthbert goes along with this?' She wondered once again what she ever saw in the man before her.

'Why not ask him? He'll be here any minute.'

As if by magic the engine of a car could be heard. There was silence in the room as a car door slammed shut and footsteps could be heard approaching. The door opened and there stood Charles Cuthbert, grey-haired, round-bellied, wearing an expensive business suit. He looked at Josh and then at Megan before returning his gaze to Josh. 'So you're the man who's been causing me a lot of trouble,' he said, his lips a grim line.

'Trouble you brought on yourself, but glad I could oblige,' said Josh.

Charles Cuthbert gave a short snigger. 'Pity it's got to end for both of you.

Lucky for me whatever you've found out hasn't been passed on to Blackstone.'

'How would you know?'

His face darkened and he looked over at Marcus. 'Because my good friend here assures me he knows nothing. Robert Blackstone and I go back a long way. He'd just love to see my business go down the drain. Always imagined he was better than me even when we were at school together. Always popular, won everything on the sports field and was top of the class when we took exams.' He pointed his finger at Josh. 'But not this time. This time I'm the winner.' A smirk crossed his face.

Josh realised the man was enjoying every minute of this.

Cuthbert turned to Terry. 'Take them to the container. It's due to go overseas in the morning and by the time they're discovered it will be too late.' He looked at Josh and Megan. 'Sorry it was such a short acquaintance but I have deals to do and money to make.'

He chuckled as he left the room.

Megan, who'd kept quiet from the moment Charles Cuthbert entered the room suddenly came to life. 'Let us go, Marcus. Someone is bound to discover we're missing and come looking for us.'

'Of course they will,' he said, grabbing her arm. He gestured to Terry to move over to Josh. 'But as Charles said, by then it will be too late.'

Megan gave him a cold stare. 'What did I ever see in you?'

Before Marcus could answer, the sound of police sirens could be heard in the distance and they were getting louder and louder!

Marcus look surprised, but then panic crossed his features. 'How on earth . . . ? Come on Terry, it's the cops, let's get out of here!' he shouted letting go of Megan and turning to the door.

Megan was having none of it. She was angry and the idea of Marcus escaping didn't sit well with her. Thinking quickly, she looked round the room and grabbed hold of a piece of wooden shelving propped up against the wall near her. She swung it towards the back of Marcus's legs. It caught him square on, causing his knees to buckle and he fell to the floor.

Terry, taken by surprise moved towards Marcus. Josh took the opportunity to knock the gun out of his hand. It skidded across the floor as he wrestled with the bigger man. They fell on the floor together, fists flying. Terry managed to shove Josh off him and reached for the gun, pointing it at Josh.

Megan seeing Josh in trouble let go of Marcus.

'No way!' she shouted, swinging the piece of wood at Terry's hand. The gun exploded just as it was knocked from his hand.

Josh fell to the ground with a groan.

Megan screamed.

The police burst through the door to find Megan launching herself at Terry, her fists pounding into his chest.

'Get this woman off me!' he squealed as she raked her nails down on his cheeks. As the police pulled her off she looked down at Josh who lay on the floor his eyes closed. She shrugged off the police officer and knelt beside Josh. There was a red stain on his shoulder –blood from a gunshot wound. He was mumbling, coming in and out of consciousness.

'I love you, Josh. Don't you dare leave me,' she whispered, brushing his lips with her own.

His eyes fluttered open and he looked at her. 'Say that again,' he whispered.

'Don't you dare leave me,' she repeated.

'No, the other bit before that.'

She managed a smile. 'I love you.'

'Back at you, kid,' he whispered wincing at the pain in his shoulder.

Megan laughed at his very bad impression of Humphrey Bogart before she burst into tears. She'd never expected that, when she joined the detective agency, she would end up facing the barrel end of a gun and the man that she now accepted she loved taking a bullet in the shoulder!

She watched in a haze as Marcus and Terry were led away, and then one of the policeman touched her arm.

'Miss, you need to let him go. The ambulance is here to take him to hospital.'

She looked down at Josh, hadn't noticed that her arms were wrapped around him. She reluctantly let him go. She dropped a kiss on his forehead and stood up.

The nightmare was over.

★ ★ ★

'You'll have to go home sometime,' Megan said as she snuggled up to Josh on the lumpy sofa in her living room. It was two days since Marcus was arrested along with Charles and Terry Cuthbert. Having spent two days in hospital Josh was released that morning.

'Just another couple of hours,' he whispered, pulling her closer and dropping a kiss on her head. 'I'm not sure I can cope with my mother fussing any more than she already has.'

Megan chuckled. Marie, once she'd

heard about Josh being shot, had arrived at A&E demanding to see her son. From the moment she'd seen him in the hospital bed, his shoulder wrapped in bandages she began to fuss and hadn't stopped since! Megan tried not to laugh when his mother combed his hair and patted his pillows, even held a cup with a straw to his mouth when he wanted a drink. He'd put up with it because he loved her but Megan could tell that the constant attention was wearing him down. So Megan had suggested that he spend a couple of hours with her before going home. Josh immediately took her up on her suggestion, assuring his mother it would only be for a few hours.

They needed to talk. That was impossible with his mother fussing, and the doctors, nurses and even the police constantly interrupting them. Then Sarah arrived. It turned out that it had been her who'd called the police when she saw them being loaded into a car at gun point.

'Thank goodness I invited you round

for a girly night in,' Megan said as she hugged her friend.

'So where do we go from here?' Josh said now, catching a lock of her hair in his fingers.

'Well, the police want us to go to the station and make a formal statement. We need to speak to Robert Blackstone and tie up loose ends on the case.'

The man had phoned Josh as soon as he'd heard about the drama, wanting to assure himself that Josh hadn't sustained any lasting damage. He was out of the country at present but would meet up with both of them on his return.

'No, I don't mean about the case. I mean us. We haven't talked about . . . our feelings.' He pulled back a little and looked into her eyes. 'I do love you, Megan. I wasn't just saying it in the heat of the moment, and I'm sure you weren't either.'

'No, I wasn't. I meant every word.'

'Good,' he said, pulling her closer and kissing her. He intended it to be just a soft butterfly kiss but it turned into something stronger and they only pulled apart when they were both breathless.

'You haven't answered my question,' he said softly. 'Where do we go from here?'

'I think it would be a good idea if we let our relationship take its natural course. After all, you might not like my cooking.' There was a twinkle in her eye as she spoke.

Josh chuckled. 'Sarah's told me all about your cooking — or rather lack of it. No worries, we can always eat out.'

'We could, but your mother has offered to give me lessons.'

'Well, that's all sorted then,' he said, pulling her close again and going in for another kiss.

20

Megan turned to Josh as they walked down the steps of the Court house together. 'It's finally over,' she said.

It had been nine months since that terrible night and today they'd watched as Marcus Rowland and the Cuthberts were found guilty of kidnapping, along with charges of theft and fraud.

Megan watched her ex-boyfriend from the witness box as she gave her evidence.

No longer was Marcus the brash and confident kidnapper. Instead here stood a man who seemed to shrink as she gave her testimony. He held his head down and didn't glance at her for one second.

She didn't feel sorry for him, but the same couldn't be said for his mother. Her heart went out to the woman who'd turned up every day and wept into her handkerchief as the evidence revealed that her son wasn't the man she brought up. Life could be so cruel.

Their kidnapping and the subsequent arrests not only hit the headlines in the local paper but also the national papers, helping to put their detective agency on the map and creating more business for them. They were now considering hiring a receptionist to help with the everyday clerical work.

Most importantly Josh and Megan had the time they needed to get to know each other better and their romance raced along — until a month ago when he'd surprised her . . .

She should have guessed something was happening when he had arrived at her door one Saturday morning and told her there was something he needed to show her. She had followed him downstairs as he led her outside.

'What do you think?' he'd said, tilted his head towards the plaque on the wall that read:

Mr & Mrs Rayne — Detective Agency.

She had turned to Josh, who instantly dropped on one knee, holding a ring box in his hand. He opened it to reveal a single diamond, nothing flashy, just simple which suited her.

'Am I being a little ahead of myself?' he'd said, his brown eyes that once glittered with anger now softened with love.

Deciding to tease him just a little she looked at the sign, and then at Josh, and then back to the sign.

'Megan?' He had sounded anxious when she didn't answer.

At last she turned back to him with a wide smile on her face. 'Yes! Of course!' she cried holding out her hand.

He had slipped the ring on her finger before pulling her into his arms, his lips meeting hers.

Now, she looked down at her left hand and the diamond sparkling on her finger, and a shiver of delight ran through her.

'I feel that at long last I can relax,' Megan said as they walked towards the car park.'

Josh took her hand. 'And that's just what you're going to do,' Josh said tugging her along the path. 'Just think, in two weeks we'll be on a plane heading for our honeymoon destination.'

She smiled at him. 'Our honeymoon. Can you believe all that's happened in the last few months? I mean, nine months ago we were at each other's throats and now look at us, ready to start a whole new life together.'

'The best decision I ever made was deciding to keep you as my partner.'

Megan gave him an indignant look before digging him in the ribs. 'Hey, I think you've got your facts wrong. Weren't you the one who was going to buy me out when you had the money? I'll never forget the look of horror on your face when the solicitor read out Uncle Ronald's will.'

Josh laughed and held up a hand in defence. 'I might have been a little hasty,' he admitted, 'But you got under my skin and it didn't take long to fall in love with you.'

So much was happening at the moment. Once Josh had said he loved her he didn't think it was necessary to wait to get married. Megan wondered if it was too soon but he insisted that they'd waited long enough. They came to a compromise. They'd wait until after Marcus's court case. As Megan said, she would never feel comfortable until she knew for certain the man was out of their lives for good.

Josh looked at his watch. 'Come on or we'll be late for the party,' he said as they reached their parked car.

As they drove along the road, Megan thought how lucky she was to have found Josh. They were a perfect match even though she still sometimes got angry with him if he forgot to tell her things she needed to know, but that was Josh and she doubted she would ever change him. But then she didn't want to — he was, in her eyes, perfect.

★ ★ ★

Today there was another important event. It was Lily Frampton's birthday.

'Lily looks so much better,' Megan commented as they pulled up in front the Frampton's house.

'She does,' Josh agreed. He stepped out of the car and followed Megan up the pathway.

Balloons were hanging from the front door and he heard laughter coming from inside the house.

Megan rang the bell and the door was immediately opened.

'We wondered where you'd got to,' a worried Allison said as she stood in the doorway. 'Did everything go alright today?' Like everyone else, the Framptons had read about the kidnapping.

'As we expected,' Josh said as they stood on the doorstep.

'That's great news,' Allison said, the worry leaving her face. 'Come on, we've been waiting to get the party started and we couldn't do that until the guests of honour arrived.'

The small house was crowded with family and friends. They all clapped as Megan and Josh walked into the room.

Lily sat in the centre looking so different from the sick little girl of nine months before. Gone were the purple shadows around her eyes, her skin no longer grey but a healthy pink and there was a sparkle in her eyes.

The tests on Sheila were successful. She was a match and the treatment was carried out as quickly as possible. Lily started to improve almost immediately much to her parent's relief.

'We can't thank you enough,' Allison said now as she watched her daughter laughing and joking with one of her cousins.'

'We're only glad that it turned out right for you,' Josh assured her.

Megan walked over to Lily. 'How's the colouring going?' she asked.

'Great thanks, Megan,' Lily said with a smile.

'Good, because Josh and I decided that because you enjoyed it so much last time, you deserved another present.'

She looked over at Josh who produced a box from behind his back.

'Hope you like it,' he said placing it on her lap.

Lily looked at the gaily wrapped parcel and like any young girl attacked the wrapping paper with gusto. Inside was an enormous painting palette containing every colour imaginable. She held it up and looked over at her parents.

'Look Mum, just what I wanted!' She wrapped her arms first around Josh and then Megan and thanked them for their gift.

Sheila walked over to them, smiling. 'I just want to thank you again for finding me. I've been such a fool all these years.' She glanced over at Lily as she showed her cousins her painting set. 'I know now what I've been missing all this time. Not having children didn't seem to bother me, but seeing Lily when she was so sick made me think that I should have been there for her long before now. If I had, perhaps she wouldn't have suffered so much.'

Megan rested a hand on the other woman's arm. 'You're here now and that's all that matters.'

'True, and thankfully it's turned out

alright. We were all prepared for the results to be negative so it was such a relief when we heard the good news. Brian and I have decided to come and live near here for a while. We've put off our travels for another twelve months at least. We need to spend more time with the family.' Sheila looked over at her niece. 'She's so looking forward to your wedding and being a bridesmaid.'

Josh and Megan had talked it over. They didn't want a big wedding, just family and a few friends, but one thing they did want was for Lily to have the experience of being a bridesmaid. Her delight when they'd asked her was just the best thing! She'd even drawn a picture of the bridesmaid dress she wanted and Megan had scoured the shops looking for something as near to it as possible which received the little girl's approval.

'It's the least we can do after all she's gone through. It's an honour for both Josh and myself that she's agreed.'

Sheila chuckled. 'Wild horses wouldn't have stopped her! She so excited, Allison tells me she hasn't stopped talking about it and has even been practising walking down the aisle. I also wanted to thank you for the invitation for both Brian and myself. I'm not sure we deserve it after the run-around you had trying to find me.'

'All in a day's work, and we're delighted that you've accepted the invitation.' She laughed. 'If it wasn't for you, Josh and I wouldn't have spent so much time together and fallen in love.'

They chatted for a few minutes, Sheila telling her that Lily enjoyed her first trip on a canal boat a few weeks ago.

Megan stood by Josh, their fingers entwined. 'Everything has turned out just right hasn't it?' she whispered in his ear.

Allison appeared with the birthday cake, candles shaped as coloured pencils were alight much to Lily's delight. She blew out the candles as everyone sang *Happy Birthday*.

★ ★ ★

'The end of a perfect day,' Josh said later that evening as he handed Megan a glass of red wine. They were at her newly decorated flat. Gone was the 80's décor and the lumpy sofa, now replaced with soft blues and creams and a comfy settee.

'I'm glad we've decided to live here,' she said taking a sip of her wine.

'Me too.'

He went to pull her into his arms when his mobile bleeped. He pulled it from his pocket and read the message. He smiled, holding up his phone for Megan to read the words.

All aboard the Ocean Experience — *both mothers have their sea legs. Be back in time for the wedding.*

Megan laughed. 'They're both getting on so well,' she said. 'I just hope that Marie has taken some earplugs with her, because my mother will talk her to death! I'm not sure she'll manage an entire three weeks at sea with someone who's as big a chatterbox as my mum!'

Josh wrapped his arms around her and kissed the top of her head.

'She'll be fine. I've not seen her so happy in a long time, to be honest. When I dropped them off at the station yesterday they were discussing which cruise to take next!'

'Talking of holidays. You still haven't told me where we're going for our honeymoon.'

'And I'm not going to. My lips are sealed. It's a surprise.'

'But what am I supposed to pack?'

He looked serious for a moment. 'I don't care what you pack, just as long as you're there. I love you, Megan, and from now on I'm going to keep you safe from harm. No way are you going to have a gun pointed at you ever again.'

He shuddered at the memory.

She hugged him tightly, loving how he cared for her so much.

'But you haven't answered my question. If you don't tell me where we're going, how am I supposed to know what I need to pack?'

'You're the detective, so work it out!' he said, his lips twitching with supressed laughter. 'But a bikini might be a good idea.'

'Oh, I think that can be arranged,' she murmured just before he kissed her.